Ivy could tell by the crinkles at his temples that he was smiling—but what kind of a smile it was, she didn't know.

She didn't want to. Just one look at those eyes made her gut contract in a sizzling, heat-filled clutch. She wondered what it would be like to wake up to those eyes, that skin… Or what would have happened in that lift yesterday if she hadn't pulled away.

She was darned glad she *had* pulled away… frustrated, but glad.

But what if she hadn't? Would he have kissed her? And why? Why her when there were so many beautiful women for him to kiss?

My God. Her mouth dried. She couldn't be thinking like that. She couldn't be imagining what it would be like to have Matteo touch her. To kiss him… Not when someone's life was on the line—although, thank goodness, not in her hands.

Not at all. She wasn't the kind of girl to have flings and she didn't want anything else. Didn't even want a fling… Unless…

No. Not a fling. Not with Matteo Finelli.

Dear Reader,

Thank you so much for picking up Matteo and Ivy's story.

The idea for this book came from a news article I read about a doctor getting into trouble for commenting about a case on social media. The dos and don'ts of stepping into that very public place, the internet, as a professional person intrigued me. What if someone did something silly and inadvertently brought their place of work into the glare of the media? What would the ramifications be? How do medical providers deal with social media platforms? And, best of all, how would a very English uptight hospital lawyer deal with a super-sexy, rule-breaking Italian man?

These two professionals with very different approaches to life have no idea what's about to hit them when Ivy summons Matteo to her office for a dressing-down!

Both of them have been hurt before, and neither wants to trust anyone any time soon—but having to live a little in each other's world opens them up to the potential of letting their guards down and falling in love. And they fight it every step of the way.

Matteo and Ivy were such fun to write about— possibly my favourite characters so far (although I always think that!). But what's not to like about a handsome Italian surgeon and a good old feisty Yorkshire lass? (I'm slightly biased, I know…)

For all my writing news and release dates visit me at louisageorge.com

Happy reading!

Louisa x

TEMPTED
BY HER
ITALIAN SURGEON

BY
LOUISA GEORGE

MILLS
BOON

First published in Great Britain 2015
by Mills & Boon, an imprint of Harlequin (UK) Limited,
Large Print edition 2015
Eton House, 18-24 Paradise Road,
Richmond, Surrey, TW9 1SR

© 2015 Louisa George

ISBN: 978-0-263-25513-3

Printed and bound in Great Britain
by CPI Antony Rowe, Chippenham, Wiltshire

A lifelong reader of most genres, **Louisa George** discovered romance novels later than most, but immediately fell in love with the intensity of emotion, the high drama and the family focus of Mills & Boon Medical Romance.

With a Bachelor's Degree in Communication and a nursing qualification under her belt, writing medical romance seemed a natural progression and the perfect combination of her two interests. And making things up is a great way to spend the day!

An English ex-pat, Louisa now lives north of Auckland, New Zealand, with her husband, two teenage sons and two male cats. Writing romance is her opportunity to covertly inject a hefty dose of pink into her heavily testosterone-dominated household. When she's not writing or researching Louisa loves to spend time with her family and friends, enjoys travelling and adores great food. She's also hopelessly addicted to Zumba®.

Books by Louisa George

A Baby on Her Christmas List
200 Harley Street: The Shameless Maverick
How to Resist a Heartbreaker
The Last Doctor She Should Ever Date
The War Hero's Locked-Away Heart
Waking Up With His Runaway Bride
One Month to Become a Mum

Visit the Author Profile page at millsandboon.co.uk for more titles.

Praise for
Louisa George

'*How to Resist a Heartbreaker* keeps you hooked from beginning to end, but make sure you have a tissue handy, for this one will break your heart only to heal it in the end.'
—*HarlequinJunkie*

'A moving, uplifting and feel-good romance, this is packed with witty dialogue, intense emotion and sizzling love scenes. Louisa George once again brings an emotional and poignant story of past hurts, dealing with grief and new beginnings which will keep a reader turning pages with its captivating blend of medical drama, family dynamics and romance.'

—*GoodReads* on
How to Resist a Heartbreaker

'Louisa George is a bright star at Mills & Boon, and I can highly recommend this book to those who believe romance rocks the world.'

—*GoodReads* reader review on
How to Resist a Heartbreaker

CHAPTER ONE

'WHAT ON EARTH…?' Ivy Leigh blinked at the image downloading to her inbox, pixel by tiny pixel.

A…bottom?

A beautiful perfectly formed, tanned, bare bottom. Two toned thighs, a sculpted back…a naked male body, in what looked like a men's locker room. A tagline next to the pert backside read: *Dr Delicious. As perfect as a peach. Go on…take a bite.*

She swallowed. And again. Fanned her hot cheeks. She might have imposed a strict dating hiatus but she still had an appreciation of what was fine when she saw it. But why on earth would her work computer be the recipient of such a thing?

Maybe the spam screens on the hospital intranet server weren't up to scratch. Adding a new note to her smartphone to-do list—*Call IT*—she let out a heat-infused sigh that had nothing to do with sexual frustration and everything to do with this new job. Two weeks in and yet another department she needed to pull into order. Still, she'd been employed here to drag this hospital into the twenty-first century and that was what she was going to do, no matter how many toes she trod on.

Twisting in her chair to hide the offending but not remotely offensive bottom from anyone who might walk past her open office door, she sneaked a closer look at the image, her gaze landing on a pile of what looked like discarded clothes on a bench. No, not clothes as such…

Scrubs?

Please, no.

Dark green scrubs bearing the embroidered name of St Carmen's Hospital. She gasped, and whatever vague interest she'd had dissolved into a puddle of professional anxiety…her bordering-on-average day was fast turning bad.

So who? What? Why? *Why me?*

She slammed her eyelids shut and refused to look at the accompanying email message.

Okay, big girls' pants.

Opening one eye, she took a deep breath and read.

From Albert Pinkney. St Carmen's Hospital Chairman. His formidable perfectly English pronunciation shone through his words. 'Miss Leigh, what in heaven's name is this? Our new marketing campaign? Since when did St Carmen's turn into some sort of smutty cabaret show? This is all over the internet like a rash and is not synonymous with the image we want to present. The benefactors are baying for blood. We are a children's hospital. You're the lawyer—do something. Make it disappear. Fix it.'

Because she was probably the only person who could solve this—when all else failed call in the lawyer to shut it down, or drag some antiquated law out and hit the offender with it.

And, damn it, fix it she would. Although making it disappear would be a little harder. Didn't Pinkney know that once something was out on the net, it was there for ever? Clearly he was another candidate to add to her social media awareness classes.

First, find out who this…specimen belonged

to. Now, that was going to be an interesting task. 'Becca! Becca!'

'Yes, Miss Leigh?' Her legal assistant arrived in the doorway and flashed her usual over-enthusiastic grin. 'What can I help you with?'

'Delicate issue… You've been here a while and have your ear to the ground. You must know pretty much all of the staff by now. Have you any idea who this…might belong to?' Ivy twisted away and made a *ta-da* motion with her hands towards her computer screen.

'Oh, my…' Becca fanned her face with the stack of manila folders in her hand. 'Take a bite? I'm suddenly very hungry.'

Me, too. 'That is so not the point. Can you see our logo? Right there. We can't have this sort of thing happening, it's very bad for our reputation.'

'Not unless we're trying to attract a whole tranche of new nurses… No? Wrong response? Sorry.' Becca gave a little shrug that said she wasn't sorry at all and that, in fact, she was really quite impressed. 'It's very nice. It is kind of perfect. And it says it belongs to a doctor so we can narrow it down. We could do one of those police line-ups, get the main suspects against the wall and...' She looked back at the picture, her voice breathy and high-pitched. 'I'm happy to organise that.'

'Get in line.' But, seriously, how many years at law school? For this? This was what she'd studied so hard for? This was why she'd hibernated away from any kind of social life? Her plan had always been to get into a position where she could safeguard others from what she'd had to endure, to prevent mistakes that cost people their happiness. Not chastise a naked man about impropriety. Still, no one could say her job didn't have variety. 'I don't want to narrow it down, Becca, I want it gone. We need to send out a stack of take-down notices, get the PR team onto damage limitation. And whoever put this out there is going to learn what it's like to feel the wrath of Ivy Leigh.'

It was late. The cadaver transplant he'd just finished on a ten-year-old boy had been difficult and long, but successful, with a good prognosis. He had a planned surgery list lined up for tomorrow and a lot of prep to work up. A ward round. And now this—an urgent summons to a part of the hospital he had not even known existed. Or, for that matter, cared about. The legal team? At six-thirty in the evening? Wouldn't all the pen-pushers have gone home? Matteo Finelli's mood was fading fast. He rapped on the closed door. Didn't wait to hear a response, and walked right in. 'You wanted to see me?'

'Yes.' The woman in front of him sat up straight behind an expensive-looking wide mahogany desk that was flanked by two filing cabinets. Beyond that a large window gave a view over the busy central London street. It was sunny out there and he imagined sitting in a small bar or café with the sun on his back as he downed a cold beer. Instead of being in here, doing this.

Apart from a calendar on the desk there was nothing else anywhere in the room. Nothing personalised, no photos, no pens, stapler…anything. She either had a bad case of OCD or had just moved in. Which would explain why he had not heard of her or seen her around. She ran a hand through short blonde hair that made her look younger than he'd imagined she must be to have achieved such a status and such a large office.

Cool green eyes stared at him. The blouse she wore was a similar colour—and why he'd even noticed he couldn't say. Her mouth, although some would say was pretty, was in a tight thin line. She looked buttoned-up and tautly wound and as if she had never had a moment of pleasure in her life. She met his anger with equal force. 'Mr Finelli, I presume? Please, take a seat.'

He didn't. 'I have not time. I was told you needed to see me immediately... What is the problem?'

'Okay, no pleasantries. Fine by me. I'll cut to the chase. Tell me...' The eyes narrowed a little. Her throat jumped as she swallowed. Emerald-tipped fingers tapped on a keyboard and an image flickered onto the screen. 'Is this you?'

There was no point in concealing his laugh. Whoever had taken the photo had held the lens at a damned fine angle. He looked good. More than good. He whistled on an out breath. 'You like it?'

'That's not the point.' But her pupils flared and heat hit her cheeks.

'You do like it? It is impressive, yes? And you summoned me all the way to the other side of the hospital for a slide show of naked bodies...interesting.' He turned to go. 'Now, I can leave? I have work to do.'

'Not so fast, Mr Finelli.'

Ma che diavolo? 'Call me Matteo, please.'

The woman blinked. 'Mr Finelli, why did you post this picture on the internet? Were you hoping for it to go completely viral, because, congratulations, it did. It seems that cyberspace can't get enough of your…assets. Have you any idea what damage you have caused the hospital by posing for this with the St Carmen's logo available for the world to see?'

'Everybody calls me Matteo, I do not answer to Mr Finelli—too formal. Too…English. I did not post that picture anywhere. And with all due respect, Miss…' His eyes roved over her face—which was turning from a quite attractive pink to a dark shade of red—then to her name badge. Her left hand. No wedding band. Definitely Miss. 'Miss Ivy Leigh. I was not posing.'

'Do you deny this is your bott…er…*gluteus maximus*?'

It wasn't fair to smile again. But he did. 'Of course I don't deny it. I've already agreed that it is mine. But clearly I did not take the picture and I did not pose. It looks to me like I'd had a shower, I was stretching to get my clothes out of the locker, with my back to the lens, you cannot see my face. I can't take a photo of the back of my head from that distance, can I? Besides which I am a very busy doctor and I do not have time to sit around playing on the internet like some people.' *Like you*, he thought. But he let that accusation hover in the silence. 'I don't know for sure who took the picture, but I can guess.'

'Oh? Who?' She leant forward, her eyes fixed on his face, eyebrows arched. In another lifetime it might have been fun to play a little more with her. To see where her soft edges were, if she had any. But not in this life.

'Ged Peterson.' *Touché, my man. You win this round.* 'My registrar, he loves playing pranks.'

'Peterson. Peterson. Ged? Short for Gerard?' Those green-tipped fingers tapped into some database on the computer. 'He doesn't work here.'

'No. But he did. Until last month when he went to work in Australia. He said he was going to give me a leaving present. I didn't realise it would be this.' Matteo stepped back, primed to leave. 'And now we have solved the mystery I must go.'

'Absolutely not. Stay right there.'

That got his attention. No woman had ever spoken to him like that before. It was…well, it was interesting. 'Why?'

'Again, I ask you; have you any idea of the damage you have caused? Lady Margaret has withdrawn her funding for the new family rooms in protest already. Parents are complaining that this is not what they expect from an institution responsible for their children's lives. Surgeons who complain about being overworked and underpaid and yet have time to flaunt their bodies make us look ridiculous. It's not professional.'

'Everyone needs to stop overreacting. It is nothing.'

With a disdainful look that suggested he was in way over his pretty little head, she shook hers. 'Image is everything, Mr Finelli. In this technological age it's all about the message we send out to gain trust and respect. We need people on side to volunteer, raise funds, hit targets. We do not need some jumped-up surgeon flashing his backside with our logo in the picture.'

He strode forward and leaned towards her, pointing at the picture getting a nose full of honeysuckle scent in the process. Overly officious she might be, but she smelt damned good. He edged away from the perfume because it was strangely addictive and he didn't need any more distractions today. This was enough and he still had a few hours' work ahead of him. 'If you are worried about funding I have an idea…why not take another eleven pictures of me and make some calendars you hospital administrators all seem to love so much? Sell me?'

'I am a lawyer.' As if that explained anything. Actually, it explained a lot. With one brother already qualified and another working his way through college, Matteo knew that law school was just as rigorous as med school. That those dark shadows under her eyes weren't from late nights drinking in bars but from studying into the early hours. That this woman had worked diligently amidst strong competition. Along with her English-rose complexion and porcelain skin, it also explained that she'd probably spent the best part of her life cooped up indoors with her nose in a book, not exploring the world, not simply lying in the last rays of a relaxing afternoon letting the sun heat your skin. It explained why she was so damned coiled.

She shook her head. 'The money you've already

lost us is in the thousands, possibly hundreds of thousands, Mr Finelli. Calendars only make a few pounds per copy.'

'With my backside on them it would make a lot more.'

'You really do have a high opinion of yourself, don't you?' Her voice had deepened and he got the feeling she was trying very hard to be calm.

Good, because that meant he was niggling her, probably not as much as she was niggling him… but, well, he had more important things to do. Like go check on the transplant patient. 'Sure. Why not?'

In what he could only describe as a power play she stood up and walked around the desk. If he wasn't mistaken it took her a moment to steady herself, then she grabbed a file from a filing cabinet and slammed it shut with finesse and flair. She sat back down again, but not before he'd taken a good long look at the cinched-in waist, curve-enhancing, slim-legged trousers and wedge heels.

Even more interesting…

Opening what he now realised was his employment file, she gave him a cold stare. 'Look, Mr Finelli, it's obvious you are not taking this issue seriously. I need to make sure you are aware of the consequences of having your naked body sprawled over the internet with our name and logo on it. I have discussed the issue with the HR department and the chairman and we are all in agreement that we need to instigate some courses for the staff on the whys and wherefores of social media etiquette. These will be mandatory for every—'

'Because of this? I did nothing wrong.'

'Because of this. Because we can't run risks with people's lives, or be distracted from our true purpose as a hospital. Because we can't make mistakes. Distraction causes death or damage.' This was clearly very important to her—personal, maybe, judging by the passion in her eyes and the slight shake in her hands.

She took a sip of water from a glass next to her elbow. And didn't, he noticed, offer him anything to drink. She waited a moment and seemed to settle herself before continuing. 'We have to control how we are seen, and this episode has just cemented my point. I ran the classes very successfully at my last place of employment and am starting them here on Thursday. You will be required to attend.'

No way. 'I operate on Thursdays.'

'And Tuesdays and Fridays. I know. There are only four sessions. You will be expected to attend them all, like every other person in this hospital, then no more will be said about the matter.'

Dio santo. She was serious. 'Have you any idea how precious operating theatre time is to a surgeon?'

She looked away and her eyes flickered closed for a moment. Then she gathered herself together. 'I have some understanding, yes.'

'And if I refuse?'

She tapped his folder. 'You will have to face a disciplinary hearing. Then there will be no operating time at all. It will be time-consuming and messy. There may even be a stand-down period. Who can say?'

Now the niggling descended into outright anger. 'On what grounds?'

'Bringing the organisation into disrepute. Refusing mandatory training. It's all quite clear in the employment contract…expected behaviour, training requirements, dress code, et cetera. Mr Finelli, many hospital boards don't allow their physicians to have a public face on social media. We are not unusual in wanting to protect ourselves.'

Round one to Ivy Leigh. Ivy…wasn't there a plant…poison ivy? *Sommaco velenoso*. It described her perfectly. He just needed a counter argument to bring Poison Ivy down a peg or two. 'Perhaps I could sue you too.'

Now her eyes widened with a flicker of nervousness. 'What the hell for?'

'Breach of my privacy. I could suggest that I did not give my permission for my body to be used in such a poorly contrived advert.'

She laughed and it was surprisingly soft and feminine. 'Go on and indulge yourself in any fantasy you like. But you and I both know this was not an advert. You have no grounds, but I do. In fact, section three of the Workplace—'

'Forget it. I'm not listening any more. I will not attend your sessions.'

'Okay. Your choice.' She reminded him of his younger sister, Liliana, who would not give up. Ever. Arguing with her was like arguing with a brick wall. 'Then I will have to invite you to attend a meeting with our human relations director first thing tomorrow morning.'

'No.' Take more time out of his work schedule? Maybe Mike would swap his cardiac roster from a Wednesday for one week just to make this in-sufferable woman go away?

'Mr Finelli, we are both on the same side.'

'Like hell we are.' But he did not have any more time to waste on this. Better to get it over and done with. 'You leave me with no choice. I'll do the four sessions.'

'Then it's sorted. After that you won't hear any-thing more from me on this matter. Thank you for your time.' She put out her hand and, grimly, he shook it. It was warm and firm and confident. And a little something reverberated through his body at her touch—which he steadfastly ignored. Clearly she felt none of it as her voice remained calm and cool, like her eyes. 'I'm sure you'll find the sessions most interesting.'

'I'm sure I won't. Now I need to rearrange my day. Four sessions shouldn't take up much time. I will be free from what time? Lunch?'

Amusement flashed across her features, as if she'd won a well-fought victory. 'Oh, sorry, didn't I make myself clear? By four sessions I meant four days.'

'Four days? No. No way. I'm not doing it.'

'But you agreed. And we shook hands. Is an Italian man's word as good as his honour?'

He held her gaze. His honour was fine and intact, unlike others he could name. He would never betray anyone the way he had once been betrayed. 'It is. But I have one condition.'

'Oh, yes?' Her expression told him she thought he was not well placed to be making conditions.

'For every minute I have to spend in your ridiculous class you have to spend an equal amount of time with me, doing my work. The work this hospital is so famous for doing. Saving lives. Then perhaps you'll see just how badly you have wasted my time.' He held her gaze. Saw the flicker of anxiety stamped down by determined resolve as she nodded.

'Okay.' Her smile was like condensed milk—way too sweet. 'Seeing as I'm new to the hospital, I have to familiarise myself with each department anyway. And it'll give me invaluable insights into the specific kind of legal issues that could arise there and a chance to review policy. This way I'll be killing two birds with one stone.'

How had he thought it might be fun to play with her? Fun was over. This was war. 'Believe me, Miss Leigh, the only killing going on in my OR is of your determination to make a damned fool of me. Goodbye.'

CHAPTER TWO

HE WASN'T GOING to come.

Ivy surveyed the conference room filled with porters, nursing staff, ward clerks and doctors, all chattering and drinking copious cups of coffee before the first session started in less than two minutes. And why the heck, with a room full of attendees who looked interested and invested in learning about social media, she was shamefully disappointed that she couldn't see Mr Finelli's famous backside in the foray, she couldn't fathom. Only that she now appeared to be locked in some sort of battle of wills with the doctor and she'd been looking forward to showcasing her side and proving her very valid points. The man may have been infuriatingly narcissistic but she'd believed him a worthy adversary. Clearly not. Typical that he hadn't bothered to turn up.

Mind you, with those dark Mediterranean eyes, that proud haughty jaw and thoughts of what was under those scrubs, it was probably a good thing. And it would be hard to concentrate on her talk with that glower searing a hole in her soul.

'Okay, Miss Leigh…' Becca handed her the folders of hand-outs for the participants. 'One each and a few to spare. Morning tea's at ten-thirty. Catering will deliver at about ten-fifteen.'

'And lunch? You know how these things go. If they don't get regularly fed and watered they get grouchy.'

'One o'clock. In the Steadman Room. Oh, and the laptop's all set up with the projector, you're good to go. Good luck.'

Excellent. Everything was running perfectly, apart from a niggle of a headache. 'Thanks, and, Becca, please, please, drop the formality and call me Ivy. I know the last incumbent had you calling him sir, but I do things differently.'

'Okay. If you're su…' Her assistant's face grew a deep shade of puce as her gaze fixed on something over Ivy's shoulder. 'Oh… Just, oh.'

'Are you okay?'

'Oh, yes. Just *peachy*. Such a shame he's a break-your-heart bad boy.' Becca grinned, and moved forward as if levitated and as if breaking your heart was some kind of spectator sport and he was the *numero uno* world champion title-holder. Which he probably was. 'Mr Finelli, please grab a coffee first and then take a seat. Let me show you where the cups are.'

Great. For some reason Ivy's heart jigged a little. First-time nerves, probably. She was always jittery at the beginning of a workshop. There was so much to think about…technology not working, correct air-conditioning levels—too hot and everyone fell asleep, too cold and no one could concentrate—snacks arriving on time, holding everyone's attention, keeping track…

Suddenly he was walking towards her. She imagined Becca would think him hot, all brooding chocolate-fudge eyes and unruly dark hair. But Ivy had switched off her sexy radar years ago when she'd learned that men wanted their women perfect, and that she didn't fit that bill. Since then she'd watched her flatmates have their hearts broken and her mother reduced…just less, diminished somehow…because of a man—and Ivy had decided she wasn't going there. Give her books and her career any day. There was something perfect about a beginning, a middle and an end of a novel—a whole. Complete. And, truth be told, reading was just about all she had the energy to do after a day's work.

Unlike the other consultants, he'd adopted informal dress—no suit and tie for Dr Delicious of peachy-bottom fame. Just a white T-shirt over formidable shoulders, with dark jeans hugging slender hips. The same uniform she'd seen on every youth in Florence when she'd been there on a weekend break. She imagined him with dark aviator sunglasses on, perched on a moped like something out of a nineteen-fifties movie. Then her mind wandered back to that picture of him naked, and the knowledge of exactly what was under that uniform made her feel strangely uncomfortable. Heat shimmied through her. It was unseasonably warm in here—a spring heatwave, perhaps? Too many bodies in such a small room? She must ask someone to fiddle with the air-con at once.

Where was she? Ah, yes, keeping…what? Keeping track. *Focus.*

'Good morning, Miss Leigh. And so it begins.' Oh…and then there was the accent. Kind of cute, she supposed. If you were Becca and easily taken in by deep honeyed tones melting over your skin. She let it wash right over her, along with the irritated vibe that emanated from his every pore.

'Mr Finelli, glad you could eventually join us. I hear you kicked up a bit of a fuss about it all, though.'

A frown appeared underneath the dark curls that fell over his forehead. 'The HR director is as enthusiastic about this as you are, it seems. Does no one in this hospital have any common sense, Miss Leigh?'

'That is exactly what I'm trying to engender with this course, but some of our staff seem to want to flaunt themselves at every opportunity. And, please, call me Ivy.'

'Ivy, ah, yes. But only if you call me Matteo. Or if you can't manage that, Matt will do. *Ivy.*' He smiled as if something other than this conversation was amusing him. He took a sip of black coffee and winced. '*Dio,* more poison. Why is coffee so bad here?'

More poison? What in hell did that mean.? Uh-oh, she could guess. 'Poison ivy? Really? Is that the best you can do? I've been hearing that since I was in kindergarten. I expected better…more…

from you, Mr Finelli. Oh, sorry, Matteo. Please, do try harder.'

He put the cup into his saucer, clearly much more insulted by his drink than her words. 'I was just seeing what it would take to wind you up—not a lot, it seems.'

She played it cool, ignoring the fluster in her gut. 'Oh, make no mistake, I'm not wound up. Just disappointed by your performance so far.'

The smile he gave her was wicked and it tickled her deep inside. 'Oh, trust me, Miss Leigh, no woman has ever been disappointed by my performance.'

Heat hit her cheeks as she realised she'd been drawn in and chewed up—worse, he was flirting and she could barely admit to herself that she was a little intrigued by someone so sure of himself. Her heart beat wildly in her chest and she willed it to slow. This sort of battleground tactic was way out of her league—flirting wasn't something she was used to. A cold, hard stare and feigned disinterest had always been enough to keep any potential lovers at bay, that and her refusal to undress in anything other than darkness. Plus a side helping of reservation had helped, and a desire to not end up like her mother.

No way would she let a man have any kind of effect on her…no way would she let *this* man have any kind of effect on her.

What she needed was to put him on side and a little off balance. She looked at his cup and wondered…maybe if she let him in on her little coffee secret he might just be so taken aback he'd sit quietly at the back of the class and listen, instead of— She could only imagine what he had in store. Creating merry hell about her subject matter. What better way to derail him than by being friendly? She leaned a little closer and whispered, 'There's a coffee shop down the road on the corner, Enrico's, great coffee. I always make sure I get one on my way into work, it keeps me going. I don't like to offend the catering staff here so I decant it into one of their cups.'

'And now we have a secret shared. Me, too. And who would have thought you could be so subversive? Maybe there is more to you than I thought.' His eyes widened and then he winked. 'Enrico's a friend, and, yes, his coffee is the best this side of the English Channel. Although that isn't hard.'

'No. I guess not.' Subversive? *Subversive?* And to her chagrin that thought made her feel damned good. Although it was a stretch even for her imagination—she'd spent the better part of her life working hard and toeing every line she found. Her gaze roved over his face, all swarthy and handsome…no, beautiful, if you were the sort to get carried away by tall, dark and breathtaking. She wasn't.

Then she caught his eye. For a second, or two, maybe more, he looked at her, those dark brown eyes reaching into her soul and tugging a little. There was something about him that was deeper than she'd imagined…something more… She was caught by the hints of honey and gold in his irises, his scent of cleanness and man, and out of the two of them she realised that she was the one a little off balance. So not the plan.

The chatter in the room seemed to dull a little and he turned away, the connection broken. Ivy took a breath. For a moment he'd almost seemed human. But then he turned back, all trace of the friendliness she'd thought she'd seen wiped clear.

His voice lowered. 'So, I am keeping my side of the bargain and here I am. I'm losing valuable operating hours so you'd better blow my damned socks off with this. I'm looking forward to you joining us tomorrow. We have a double whammy for you. In theatre one we have a live donor retrieval. And next door, in theatre two, we will be performing, for your delight and delectation, a renal—*that means kidney*—transplant on a twelve-year-old girl. I hope you've got stamina as well as balls because you're going to need it. It's going to be a long day.'

He thought she had balls? Was that a compliment? Or did he just see her as an equally worthy opponent? She hoped so. 'I am well aware of what renal means, and cardio, hepatology and orthopaedic... Throw me a word, Mr Finelli, and I'm pretty sure I'd be able to translate from medico to legal to layman and back again—I aced Latin and my mother's a GP. I won my high school creative writing prize five years in a row and my favourite subject was Classics, so I think I cover all linguistic challenges. And I've got a lot more stamina than most.' She just wasn't going to mention the teeny-weeny little fact that she was also a fully paid-up member of the hemophobia club. One speck of blood and she was on her back.

So far in her hospital career she'd been able to avoid any incidents by making sure she was never in the wrong place at the wrong time—or always getting out quickly. No way would she admit to being nervous or in any way intimidated at the prospect of watching an operation—no, two operations. A real baptism of fire. 'Actually, I'm looking forward to it.'

'Me, too.' His mouth curled into a smile that was at once mesmerising and irritating. Heat swirled in her chest and she felt an unfamiliar prickling over her skin. Maybe her sexy radar had flickered back into life?

She brushed that thought away immediately. She had more important things to deal with than wayward, unsatisfied hormones.

Because somehow between now and tomorrow she was going to have to overcome her fear of blood. Maybe a quick phone call to Mum for some anti-anxiety drugs? Hypnotherapy? Although she'd heard the best way to deal with phobias was immersion therapy, she just hadn't ever put her hand up for it.

She also had to work out how she was going to stand for eight hours straight when her doctors had distinctly advised her against doing any such thing. Never mind. That was tomorrow. Today she had another hurdle to jump.

Stepping away from him, she nodded across the room to Becca, who rang a bell, drawing everyone's attention.

'Good morning, everyone.' Ivy made sure the room was silent before she continued and stepped up to the raised area. 'Thank you so much for coming today. I have what I hope will be an enlightening presentation that will entertain you as well as teach you something. I hope you don't mind if I take a seat every now and then up here on the stage—it means you get to see the slides and informative videos and not me, which I'm sure you'll all agree is preferable.'

In keeping with the presentations skills she'd honed over the years she ensured she made eye contact with as many people as possible. When her gaze landed on Matteo he looked straight back at her from his front-row seat, teasing and daring lighting up his eyes, but she had no idea what was going through his mind. She had no way of reading him, but she got the distinct impression he was weighing her up, his scrutinising gaze making her catch her breath.

Bring it on, Matteo Finelli, she tried to tell him right back. She was ready for this. *Bring it on.*

This was just the beginning.

'To recap, we have a social media policy for three main reasons: protecting patient confidentiality; protecting and promoting our brand; and protecting our staff. Be very sure that what you say is how you want to be seen, and remember that if something you put up on networking sites can be connected with St Carmen's or our patients in any way then that may result in disciplinary action. There is a lot of chatter out there and how we present ourselves is extremely important; it's very hard to erase a message or a footprint once it's out. These things have a habit of coming back to bite us in the proverbial behind.'

Matteo watched as Ivy's eyes flicked to him and he felt the sting of her retort. Okay, so having his behind out there for all the world to see hadn't been the wisest idea his friend had had, and Matteo was starting to understand a little of the ruckus it had caused. St Carmen's had a solid reputation for putting children first and he could see that having a connection with a naked man may well have done some damage. But, really, four sessions to get that message across? What in hell could next week's workshop be about?

Poison Ivy was certainly passionate about her job, he'd give her that. And her presentation skills had been first rate. He got the impression that public speaking was something she could do with finesse but that she didn't exactly love it. Her voice was endlessly enthusiastic, and he caught a hint of an accent…although not being native to England he couldn't quite place it. She certainly looked the part with another smart dark trouser suit and silk blouse—today it was a deep cobalt blue that had him reminiscing about the summer skies back home. And he felt another sting—sharp enough to remind him of the folly of thinking too hard and investing too much. And that love, in its many forms, could cut deeply.

But Ivy's ballsy forthrightness coupled with the curve-enhancing trousers and form-fitting blouse had piqued his imagination. Although why, he didn't know, she was the exact opposite of everything he usually liked in a woman. He went for tall women, and she was petite. He had a track record of tousled brunettes, and she was blonde with a...what was it? Yes, a pixie cut. He liked to entertain and enthral and she showed nothing but disinterest bordering on contempt. He wasn't usually spurned—spurning was his role. Ah, no—he never led a woman to believe he would give any more than a good time. Until the good times became more one-sidedly meaningful—and that was the signal to get out.

Putting this sudden interest down to the thrill of the chase, he nodded to her, raising his eyebrows. *Do go on.*

She gave him a disinterested smile and looked at someone else. 'I hope you've all enjoyed our journey into cyberspace and an overview of social media opportunities—as you can see, they are many and varied and more are exploding onto our screens and into our homes every day. Now that we've highlighted our hospital policy, I hope you can see how and when mistakes can be made, even from the comfort of your own sofa when you think you're engaging in a private conversation. Nothing is ever private on the internet. Next week we'll be talking about the good, the bad and the very ugly of social networking sites. In the meantime, in the words of someone much wiser than me…when it comes to the World Wide Web, don't be that person with the smartphone making dumb mistakes.'

And everyone around him seemed to have enjoyed themselves immensely. She gave a shy smile at their applause and then concentrated on logging off the laptop and clearing away her papers.

He followed the queue to the door but before he'd made it out he heard her voice. 'Mr Finelli?'

'Yes?'

She stepped down from the small stage and walked towards him, trying hard but not quite managing to hide the limp that now, at the end of a day when she'd mostly been standing, clearly gave her pain. 'I hope that was insightful?'

'It could have been a lot quicker.'

'Not everyone is as quick thinking as you.' She bit her bottom lip as if trying to hold back a smile. 'Besides, we have some very recalcitrant staff members who insist they know better than we do on these matters. I need to make sure I hammer out our message loud and clear.'

Remembering her barb, he gave her a smile back. 'I felt the hammer.'

'Good. My job here is done. I hope in future you'll be contemplating how to send positive messages that reflect the nature of our business. Or, indeed, not sending messages at all.'

'The only positive messages I need to send are in the numbers of children I and the renal department save. And in how many families don't have to endure suffering or loss of life.'

She studied him. 'Well, maybe a bit of help in drumming up support for your unit is in order? You could harness the wave, do some awareness campaigns and get…what? What is on your wish list?'

He didn't need to think twice about this—the same thing every transplant unit across the world wanted. 'More organ donors, more people willing to sign up to donate when they die. More dialysis machines. More research.'

'So put your thinking hat on and see if you can come up with a way of reaching out to people across the internet. Without taking your clothes off? There are plenty of people here in London wanting to help a good cause…but many more reaching out across the internet. Just imagine… Well, have a good evening, I'll see you in the morning. Bright and breezy.' Then she gave him a real smile. An honest to God, big smile that lit up her face. And, *Mio Dio*, the green in her eyes was intense and mesmerising. Her mouth an impish curl that invited him to join her in whatever had amused her. And something in his chest tugged. It was unbalancing and yet steadying at the same time.

'Where are you from?' For some reason his longing-to-leave brain had been outsmarted by his wanting-to-stay mouth.

Her smile melted away. 'I'm sorry?'

'Your accent. I'm not used to all the different ones yet. Other people say Landan…you say Lun-dun.'

Gathering all her gear together, she shovelled folders under one arm and carried a laptop in her hand. With a hitch of her shoulder she switched the lights out and then indicated for him to leave the conference room ahead of her while she pressed numbers into a keypad that sent the area into lockdown. 'York. I'm from York, it's in the north. A long way away. Three and a half hours' drive—on a good day.'

'Of course I have heard of it.' He noticed a slight narrowing of her eyes and her voice had dropped a little. 'And that makes you sad, being away from family?'

She shrugged. 'No. Well…yes, I suppose. You know how it is. You do miss the familiar.'

'I suppose you do.' Maybe others did. He hadn't been able to leave quickly enough and trips back home had been sporadic. Betrayal and hurt could do that to a man.

They neared the elevators and she paused, put her bag on the floor and pressed the 'up' button. 'And you? You must feel a long way from home. Which is?'

'A small village near Siena. Nothing special.'

Her eyebrows rose. 'You're joking, right? Every Tuscan village is special.'

His village was. The inhabitants, on the other hand, not so much. 'How do you know? Have you visited there?'

'Florence, that's all, just a quick weekend trip. It was lovely.' Her ribcage twisted as she tried to hitch the now falling papers back under her arm.

He reached for them, his hand brushing against her blouse, sending a shiver through his gut. Strange how his body was reacting to her. Very strange. 'Let me take those papers from you.'

'I can manage.' She stopped short and shook her head with determination and resolve, obviously trying to be strong when she didn't need to be. He got the feeling that Ivy Leigh put a brave face on a lot—to hide what? Some perceived weakness? Something that was more than a problem with her foot.

'I know you can manage. But you have too many things to carry and I have nothing. Let me take them.' Without waiting for her to answer, he took the folders and slipped them under his arm, wondering what the hell the point of this was. She was on the other side—the annoying, bureaucratic, meddling middle-men side.

Talking with the enemy, helping the enemy, whatever next? Sleeping with the enemy? Pah! As if he would do anything so foolish.

And she obviously had a full appreciation of that. 'I know what you're doing, Matteo. You're trying to get me on side and then you're going to strike. Pounce...or something. Try to catch me unawares, try to convince me to set you free from my course and then hit me where it hurts.'

'Never. I would never hit anyone.' There had been a few times when he'd come close—okay, once when he'd stepped over that line and with good reason. But never again.

She looked confused. 'Don't panic, it's a turn of phrase. I didn't mean you'd really hit me. I know you wouldn't do that.'

'Good. And, actually, I was just being nice.'

'Well, that is unexpected. Who knew you could be?'

The fleeting anger at the memories melted into humour. Ivy Leigh was good at sparring. He admired that. Always good to respect the enemy. Laughter bubbled from his chest. 'Strange, yes, considering we are on opposite sides. The next thing we know we'll be doing something ridiculous like going for a drink.'

'Oh, no. I can't do that.' She jabbed the lift button again and tsked. 'I never mix business with pleasure.'

'I'm intrigued that you think having a drink with me would be pleasurable?'

Again there was a smile, but it belied a look in

her eyes that was…half wistful, half anxious. 'I'm sure the *drink* would be very pleasurable indeed. I'm very partial to a decent red. But, as I say, it's not something I do.'

'Neither do I.'

'Then I'm glad that we agree on something.' But that wistful look remained, until she turned away.

There was no one else around. The place was silent. The conference area had all closed down for the night so it was just him and her and a buzz in the air between them that was so fierce it was almost tangible. 'And you are going where now?'

She shrugged. 'Back to the fifth floor, if this lift ever arrives. I have work to do.'

'After five o'clock? All the other paper-pushers have long gone.'

Her lips curled into a smirk. 'Pen. It's pen-pushers not paper-pushers.'

'I know, I know. I apologise. I'm still getting used to your idioms.' And she was stunning when she smiled. Which, it appeared, made him tongue-tied too. Really? What in hell was wrong with him?

'Where the hell is this lift?' Jab-jab on the button with those emerald fingernails. 'I don't think about the time I put in. I just do what's needed, and if that keeps me here all hours then so be it. Like most lawyers, I expect to work hard.'

'Then you'd make a fine doctor too.'

'Believe me, I wouldn't.' She gave a visible shudder and he wondered whether she'd been hurt at some point. Maybe a doctor had broken that well-protected heart of hers. And, again, why that was remotely relevant to anything, he didn't know.

'You don't like doctors? A hospital is a strange place to work, then.'

'Most doctors are fine. In fact, my mum's one.' Finally the lift arrived with a jolt and the doors swished open. Taking the folders from his hand, she fixed her gaze on him. 'Only a few of them ruin the reputation for the majority...'

What? As she stepped into the lift he put a hand out to stop the doors from closing. 'You mean me? *I* have a reputation?' He laughed. 'Good to know. Let me guess how that goes...I am too outspoken. I am a maverick. I am too committed to my job. Worse, I leave broken hearts in my wake...'

'Apparently so.' Her fingers tapped against the cold steel of the wall panel. 'And a lot more that I couldn't possibly say...'

'I am also very attentive to detail. Some would say passionate. I have a sense of humour. I play very hard indeed...' His gaze drifted over her face. The detail there was stunning. The eyes that gave away her emotions regardless of how hard she tried to keep them locked away. That mouth, the keeper of barbs and insults and a perfect smile. Those lips... How would it feel if he were to kiss her? How would Miss Prim and Proper react then? Would she let him see a little of what was under that hard surface? Because, dammit, he knew there was more to her. A softer side—a passionate side. Just waiting to be set free. Lucky man who ever achieved that.

The door jolted against his back, reminding him that this was neither the time nor the place to be kissing Ivy Leigh. And yet...he reached a hand to her cheek and he could have sworn he saw heat flicker across her eyes, just enough to mist them and to tell him that he was not the only one struggling with this wildly strange scenario. Her mouth opened a little, he could see her breathing had quickened, and her eyes fluttered closed for a micro-second. Enough to show he had an effect on her…and she liked it. Didn't want it, not at all, but she liked it.

She pulled away. 'So. I'll see you tomorrow. Show me what you've got, Mr Finelli, I'm expecting to be very impressed.'

He felt strongly that he could show Miss Leigh a thing or two and she'd be very impressed indeed. *Work. Work.* Reminding himself of what was truly the most important thing in his life, he took a step back too. *Che stupido.* 'Do not bring me back to that issue again. Those damned workshops. This social media thing. Miss Leigh, you make my blood boil sometimes.'

'I try my best. All part of the service.'

With that she gave him a very satisfied smile that he imagined would grace her lips at the end of a particularly heavy lovemaking session. For a fleeting second he imagined her naked and on his sheets. Spent and glowing.

'Goodbye, Mr Finelli.'

He watched the lift door swish closed, thanking the god of good timing that she'd had the good sense to put a stop to whatever dangerous game had been about to play out. She made his blood boil indeed, the heat between them had been off

the scale. No woman had made him so infuri-
ated and so turned on at the same time. He spoke
to the metal doors as the lift lurched upwards.
'Goodbye, Ivy.'

Then he turned to walk up the stairs and back to
the surgical suite. A ward round beckoned, then
some prep, allaying the fears of his patients and
their parents…then a quick gym session, a decent
meal, some sleep.

He needed to be ready for tomorrow, for Ivy
and for round two.

CHAPTER THREE

THIS IS YOUR JOB, for goodness' sake. Pull yourself together.

As long as Ivy focused on that she'd be fine. She'd put everything on the line for her job her whole adult life and had got exactly where she wanted to be: Director of Legal at a fabulous, age-old and well-respected institution. So this was just another hurdle. Just an incy-wincy hurdle that she would jump with ease.

If only for two little things…

Shut up. Blood and a bloody-minded man would not get to her. She dragged the scrubs top over her head and straightened it, leaned in to the mirror and watched her hands shake as she slid the paper hairnet hat thing over her hair, squashing her fringe in the process. *Great look, girlfriend.*

Then she took a little more notice of her surroundings. The scrubs with the St Carmen's logo and the locker room reminded her of the photo…

Would she be for ever condemned to remember that image for as long as she lived?

Half of her hoped so. The other half tried to blot it from her mind.

'Hey, Miss Leigh, are you ready?' Nancy, the OR assistant, called through the door. 'We're going in now, the surgeon's here.'

And she so hadn't needed to hear that. 'Just a second, I'm almost there.' *Okay. Breathe. Deeply. In. Out. In. Out. You can do this.* It was just a case of mind over matter. She was in control of this.

She didn't know what she was dreading most: the red stuff or the man she'd had the dirtiest dream about last night. The man she'd almost grabbed in the lift and planted a kiss on those too smug lips of his. Who she'd spent an hour trying to describe to her flatmate and had ended up with *annoyingly sexy.*

So, yes, she thought he was sexy. Just as Becca did, and, frankly, the same as all the women in the hospital did. So she was just proving she had working hormones—*nothing else to see here, move right along.* The man who was out to make her look a fool but, God knew, he might not need to try too hard, because if things didn't go as planned she'd be managing that quite well all on her own.

Popping two more herbal rescue sweets into her mouth and sucking for all she was worth, she took a couple of extra-long deep breaths and steadied her rampaging heart. Give her a sticky mediation case, two ornery barristers and an angry, justice-seeking client any day. Words...that was her thing. Words, debate, the power of vocabulary. Not medicine. Not blood. Not internal stuff. Exactly why she hadn't followed in her mother's footsteps.

Here we go.

The smell hit her first. Sharp, tangy and clinical, filling her nostrils, and she thought it might have something to do with the brown stuff a man in scrubs and face mask was painting onto the abdomen of an anaesthetised woman. Then the bright white light of the room hit her, the noise. She'd thought it would be silent—remembered only a quiet efficiency from those endless surgeries, but someone had put classical music on the speakers. It was the only soothing thing in the place.

So much for the rescue sweets. Her heart bumped along, merrily oblivious to the discomfort it was causing her, and now her hands were starting to sweat too. Someone sat at the head of the woman and fiddled with tubes. The anaesthetist, Ivy knew. She had enough experience to be able to identify most of the people in here. Another woman smiled at her and bustled past with a tray of instruments that looked like torture devices…hooks and clamps. Ivy shuddered and hovered on the periphery, not knowing what to do and feeling more and more like a spare part. Should she stand closer? But that would mean she'd get a bird's-eye view of the action.

The man painting the brown stuff raised his head and she realised it was Matteo. Matteo—she'd got to thinking of him like that. Not Mr Finelli. Not something over there and out of reach. But someone here…someone personal. Matteo. Someone she'd almost kissed, for the first time in what felt like a thousand years. All she could see of his face were those eyes, piercing, dark and direct as he looked at her. 'Ah. Miss Leigh. You're here. Come closer, please. Glad you could tear yourself away from your paper pushing.'

'Good to be here.' *Liar.*

'Nancy got you some scrubs. Good. We don't want to get your lovely office suits messed up with bodily fluids. Do come and get a better view of the procedure, my team will make space for you. I'm sorry we didn't reserve the gold-tier seating. And it's a little crowded as I need to teach as well as operate. Perhaps one day you'll be able to help us raise money for a decent viewing room? That would make all of our lives easier.'

She gave him a sarcastic smile, which she knew he couldn't see behind her mask so she stuck her tongue out instead. Then levelled her voice. 'You know very well that I'm a lawyer, not a fundraiser. However, I'll add it to your wish-list. Which is getting longer by the day.'

'I know. We surgeons are so demanding, yes? You'd think we were wanting to save lives or something.' For a moment he regarded her with humour, but it was gentle and not rude, and then he became very focused and professional. 'Okay. This patient is Emily. She's donating her left kidney to her daughter, who is twelve years old and suffers from polycystic kidney disease. Emily is a perfect match in tissue type and blood type. She's a very active lady with no medical history of any note. With one kidney she is giving her daughter the chance to have a normal life. That is, of course, as long as her body doesn't reject it, although live donors are generally better tolerated than cadaver ones. Once the kidney has been removed, I, and a team of other surgeons, will...' He paused and looked over at Ivy. 'Are you okay, standing there?'

'Yes, thanks. I'm fine.' Shifting the weight from her left foot, she eased more heavily onto her right. And then realised he was still watching her.

His eyes flicked to her feet and then back to her face. 'This is a long procedure—in fact, it's going to be a long day. Would...er...anyone like a seat?' His voice, she noted, had softened, the jokey teasing quite gone. Which was not what she wanted or expected from him. He must have noticed her limp. Goddamn. When had that been? She didn't want anyone's pity; she could hold her own as well as the next person. He called out to the orderly, 'Eric...? Do we have any chairs?'

And look weak in front of all these people. In front of her colleagues? Him? No way. She shook her head vehemently.

Matteo paused with a large green sheet in his hand. 'If you're sure? Everyone?' But she knew he meant just her. 'This is your last chance. We're going to start imminently and then we all need to concentrate.'

Oh, God. *Objection!* she wanted to shout. *Stop!* But instead she fisted her fingers into her palms, dug deep to distract herself from her raging heartbeat. 'I'm fine. Please, just do the operation.'

'As you like.' He nodded to her, the scalpel now in his hand catching the light and glinting ominously. 'Here we go, everyone. One laparoscopic donor nephrectomy begins.'

An hour later and Ivy had run out of places to look other than at the patient and risk the chance of seeing blood. She knew the right-hand corner of the room intimately now and could have recited the words on the warning sign above the electrical sockets blindfolded. The ECG monitoring machine bleeped and she focused once again on the LED display. Lots of squiggly lines and numbers. A niggly pain lodged in her lower back and her legs were starting to ache. She didn't even have anything to lean against—that would have been helpful. So she stood rooted to the spot, trying to blot out the chatter, the music, the smell. Words like tubular…renal ligament…haemo…blood. She knew that. And sorely wished she didn't.

But while her heartbeat was jigging off the scale it was clear that Matteo's wasn't. As he worked three probes jutting out from the woman's abdomen while watching his handiwork on a large TV screen, his voice was measured and calm. For all his macho Italian remonstrating, the man was a damned fine surgeon, she'd give him that. He was also a decent teacher, taking time to explain to everyone exactly what he was doing—which really was amazing. Keyhole surgery was detailed, precise and very, very clever.

Okay, so she'd misjudged him. He was not narcissistic when it mattered, he was giving of himself to his patients and to the assistants. But he was still annoying. And sexy. And had she mentioned annoying? 'We need to divide the adrenal vein so it is the optimal length for transplantation...'

She focused on the music because his running commentary was making her feel slightly woozy. Or maybe it was the heat in the room. Her gaze drifted over to him again, down his mask-covered face to his throat. The V of skin visible on his broad chest was suntanned, his forearm muscles contracting and stretching as he worked.

He stopped and arched his back, checked the screen, and, as he dipped his head to resume his work, he caught her eye. She could tell by the crinkles at his temples that he was smiling—what kind of a smile it was, she didn't know. She didn't want to. Just one look at those eyes made her gut contract in a sizzling, heat-filled clutch. She wondered what it would be like to wake up to those eyes, that skin... Or what would have happened in that lift yesterday if she hadn't pulled away.

She was darned glad she had pulled away... frustrated, but glad.

But what if she hadn't? Would he have kissed her? And why? Why her when there were so many beautiful women for him to kiss?

My God. Her mouth dried. She couldn't be thinking like that. She couldn't be imagining what it would be like to have Matteo touch her. To kiss him... Not when someone's life was on the line—although, thank goodness, not in her hands.

Not at all. She wasn't the kind of girl to have flings and she didn't want anything else. Didn't even want a fling...unless...

No. Not a fling. Not with Matteo damned Finelli. She felt her cheeks heat, shook her head to clear her mind and realised it took longer than normal for her vision to catch up. Nausea ripped through her, rising up her gut. She focused on his hands. Hands that were red with blood now. Thick and red…and… The heat in the room was toxic…and she felt cold and hot…and she could feel the blood drain from her face…

'So you are with us again? That is good.' Matteo tapped Ivy's hand with as little force as he dared muster, but enough that she'd at least open her eyes. She looked so pale, so young lying on the trolley covered with a blanket. And as she was his responsibility in the OR he'd deemed it only right to check on her. That's what he told himself anyway as she stared at him, her cheeks reddening. She started to sit up but he coaxed her back down. 'Lie still. Your blood pressure dropped and you fainted. Are you feeling okay?'

'Oh, I'm so sorry. Please, go in and finish the operation. Leave me here.' Her eyelids fluttered closed, more, he figured, out of embarrassment than feeling faint again.

People fainted in the OR on a regular basis. Nothing extraordinary. Except that this time had been the first and only time he'd felt a need to barge in and carry the victim out. But even though he had stood there helplessly as she'd fallen to the floor he'd known that he was not in a position to run to her—no matter what. His patient was his first priority. 'It is all done—it takes more than a vaso-vagal to make me leave someone on the table. You were well cared for by the recovery nurses?'

She gave him a smile. 'Yes. And I'm so sorry I took up their valuable time. It wasn't necessary and neither is this visit. You're busy.'

'Nonsense. I have ten minutes before I go into the transplant. I thought I'd better check on my unexpected patient.'

She twisted to sit up, ignoring any attempt to keep her out of harm's way. 'You didn't need to. Honestly. No one should have looked after me. I'd have been fine.'

'Oh, yes, we always leave the sick ones scattered across the OR floor like the battlefield wounded. We just step over them, like little human hurdles whenever we need to move around the room. Did you have breakfast this morning?'

'Yes.' Which was contrary to what he'd assumed

and didn't explain why a strong woman like Ivy would faint. 'A little.'

'So you fell over. Why?'

She shrugged. 'It was hot.'

'We were all hot, it gets like that. The air-conditioning is faulty—just another thing to add to my wish-list.' Maybe it had had something to do with her leg. Maybe she'd been in pain? *Pazzo*, he berated himself. Idiot. There he'd been playing games with her and she'd been unable to stand for so long. Physically unable to, for whatever reason. And he didn't want to pry into something that wasn't his business. But... 'It was something more, I think.'

She looked like she was debating how to answer. 'Okay. Yes.'

He waited for her to elucidate. 'And...?'

'I think I overdosed on rescue sweets.'

'What?' He had not been expecting that. He held back a laugh because he could see she was serious. 'Rescue sweets? Really? You were nervous about the operation? And be honest. You have the kind of face that gives away all your emotions.'

'That is not what someone of my profession

wants to hear.' She seemed to fold a little. 'It's not my usual workplace, is it?'

'Which isn't an admission of nerves, just a statement of fact.' Ever the lawyer. 'Were you scared?'

'No comment.' But her eyes dipped down and he knew he had her answer.

'So yes. What of?'

'No comment.'

'Which might work in the courts, Ivy, but won't stop me asking the questions. This is my domain now, not yours. You have a phobia? Needles? Blood? People?' *Me?* That thought made him smile even more. Because he had no doubt that Ivy believed him to be her equal. Maybe it was the buzz between them that she was afraid of. Of what that might lead to unless they both held themselves in check.

The way she pursed her lips reminded him of his sister Liliana again—reluctant to admit any kind of weakness. She'd started to look less fragile, stronger, back to her fighting self. Almost—but was that a little humility there too? 'Okay, if you must know, yes, I get a little woozy with blood...'

'Aha, so you are afraid of something. Interesting…' He'd found a weak spot. Excellent. Although seeing a young woman so pale wasn't excellent at all. Fainting in front of a group of colleagues was pretty embarrassing too, and made anyone feel washed out and often came with a thumping headache. And now he felt compelled to help her. Again. It was becoming a habit. An unusual habit that he needed to shake off. 'Okay, we'll talk about it later. I may have some suggestions to help you with that. Now, I must go and see my next client.'

'Wait. Matteo. Please.' She reached a hand to his arm and a thousand jolts rattled through him. He knew exactly what that was. Chemistry. Physics. And basic biology. There was a connection between them that overrode sense. That ignored his brain and went beyond any interest he'd felt for a woman before. What was it about Ivy Leigh that had him reacting so strongly? Why did he want to help her? What was going on with his body that this attraction was so intense, so fierce?

He wanted answers so he could stop it and get back to normal. He'd never become so interested in a woman that he'd thought about snatching a kiss at work, in an elevator. That was the stuff of romance books and definitely not for a sane, level-headed scientist like himself. He liked to have control in who he kissed...not some sort of urgent, frenzied need. Because he knew exactly where that kind of wild, irrational love got a man. And he wasn't going there ever again.

Her smile broadened. 'Thank you for your concern. But what about the transplant? I'd like to watch...from a safe distance.'

Drawing his arm away from her touch, he shook his head. 'You have nothing to prove, really. But you have to be able to hold your own in there, otherwise you become a liability, and perhaps today is a little soon for you to try to conquer your fears. So, no. You can't come in and watch. I need to make sure you are strong enough—'

'Strong? Of course I am...I was just a little overcome.'

'We don't need that kind of distraction in there. Try again next week?' By which time he'd have this snagging interest in her under control. 'I'll try to find something less intrusive for you to watch.'

Jolting upright, she fixed him with those dark green eyes. 'Damn it, I can do this.'

'Not today and that decision is final.'

Shaking her head, she lay back down on the trolley and covered her eyes with her forearm. 'So you won in the end.' She sounded disappointed but retaliatory.

'This round, yes.' Although there was less satisfaction in that fact than he'd imagined there would be.

Nancy arrived and handed Ivy a plastic cup filled with water. 'You're fine to get up now, Miss Leigh. Your blood pressure is back to normal. Why don't you have a drink first, then pop along to the locker rooms and get changed.' His OR assistant turned to him. 'Matteo, I'm sorry to interrupt, but just wanted to remind you we're having Friday night drinks tonight. Will you be coming along?'

'Of course.'

Nancy's eyes flicked over to Ivy. 'Oh, and Miss Leigh, of course. You must come too.'

Matteo guessed Nancy was playing the polite card because generally the department was pretty tight, but it would be rude not to ask her when this conversation was going on within her earshot. He ignored a little leap in his stomach at the thought of seeing her again. If that was how his body was reacting then maybe he wouldn't go tonight if she was going to be there. It was better not to fuel this attraction any further. Bad enough she'd been the first thing he'd thought about when he'd woken up this morning.

'Why does everyone insist on calling me Miss Leigh? It makes me feel like I'm a ninety-year-old spinster. Please, it's Ivy...' Ivy shook her head vehemently. 'And thanks for the offer but, no. I can't come tonight.'

Nancy chipped in. 'But we all go, every Friday, across the road to the Dragon, straight after work. It's tradition. If you work in OR it's mandatory...'

Matteo added with a grin, remembering how forceful Poison Ivy had been about attending her ridiculous course, 'And we all know what that means. No getting out of it.'

Ivy swung her legs over the edge of the trolley and straightened her scrubs, her blonde hair stuck up in little tufts, and she looked very far from the sophisticated, competent lawyer. In fact, she looked pretty damned cute all mussed up. 'But I didn't exactly do any work here, I just made a fool of myself.'

'And now you have me feeling sorry for you

all over again.' He leaned closer. Big mistake—
a nose full of her fresh scent had his senses zap-
ping into full-on alert. He stepped back again.
'Let me tell you a secret…the first day in Theatre
as a medical student, I vomited.'

'In the theatre?' Both Nancy and Ivy asked at
the same time.

He shrugged. 'No, in a bin outside. I managed
to leave just in time. A coronary bypass—messy.
It takes a bit of getting used to. There's a lot of
smells and noise and the blood…and looking inside… It's something you learn to live with. You
can't expect to be okay with seeing these things
on the first day. Luckily, you have another three
chances to get up close and personal.'

'Yay. Three.' Ivy's cheeks blazed as she drained
the cup and popped it on the table next to the trolley. 'Er…well, yes. Hypnotherapy's good, I hear.
Drugs. Total avoidance has been working really
well for me for years. But I really do need to apologise to everyone for inconveniencing them.'

'What better place to do it than at the pub?' He
couldn't believe he was convincing her to come.
'You said you needed to get to know the depart-

ments. People will chat to you more freely with alcohol in their bellies.'

'Yes,' Nancy chimed in. 'Come on, it's usually a good crowd. And if you do come I promise not to let anyone make fun of you.'

Matteo sniffed. 'Apart from me, obviously.'

'Of course, Matteo. Whatever.' With a shake of her head Nancy jabbed him in the ribs and winked at Ivy. 'Don't be taken in by him. He's just a softie really.'

'Nancy, how could you ruin my reputation?'

'Your reputation's already in tatters, my boy. We've all seen the picture... *Bite me*? Yes...oh, yes. Wouldn't we all love to do that.' Laughing, Nancy ducked away down the corridor. Leaving just him and a bed-ready Ivy, who was laughing and not making any attempt to hide it.

He gave her a smile. 'Now I definitely need you to come out tonight to fight my corner, tell them what penance I've had to serve for that damned picture. They'll be merciless.'

'This I have got to see.' Ivy patted his hand and he felt a comforting warmth that, as he looked into her sparkling eyes, transformed into a sizzle running through him. He wanted to kiss her.

Right there. To see what that mouth tasted like, how it felt slammed against his. This was a struggle he was already losing. He wanted her. As he watched her she stopped laughing, but the smile remained. 'Sorry, Matteo, it's no more than you deserve. This is one battle you'll have to fight on your own. And I don't think you'll have a hope in hell of winning.'

CHAPTER FOUR

WITH AN UNEXPECTEDLY free afternoon to attack her to-do list, Ivy felt on top of her work for the first time since she'd taken the job. Wanting to purge the embarrassment burning through her, she'd hit the tasks with gusto and now had a new to-do list that contained *complete projects*, as opposed to, *Go through the masses of unfinished stuff the useless last guy left, find out what the outstanding projects are and then complete.*

Now she had a clear idea of where she was headed—until, of course, the next crisis occurred. Because she had no doubt that it would. She could only hope it wasn't more naked photos...because that scenario appeared to get her into hotter water than she wanted to be.

She buzzed through to the next office. 'Becca, would it be possible for you to line up some interviews for me for next week?'

'Sure. Hang on, I'll come through.' Becca appeared in her office, pencil poised and notepad at the ready, as if she was about to take dictation. 'Who, what, why and when? And, please, please, let it be more bottoms to identify…peachy ones, of course.'

Ivy tried to frown, but the thought of that… *Work, girl.* 'You are incorrigible. It's proper work. You remember that? The stuff we get paid to do? Look through my diary—any time apart from Thursday and Friday. I need to take a brief on the Partridge case. So, I need to speak to…' She scanned down the list of names on the paper in front of her. 'Maggie Taylor and Leslie Anderson from Ward Three.'

Becca tapped her pad. 'That's the med negligence case, right? The feeding tube that became dislodged?'

'Yes. That hearing's coming up in a couple of weeks and I need to be apprised of all the facts.'

'Certainly. I'll organise that for you.' Becca nodded. 'But, you know, we always win anyway. Or we settle beforehand if we don't think we'll win in court.'

'Yes. I know very well how the system works.' Ivy had personal experience on both sides, but that didn't mean she liked it. Not if it meant mistakes were still being made, mistakes that could be avoided.

With this job she'd found herself in a strange place ethically—on the one hand she wanted to ensure the hospital was a safe place for all, and on the other hand she was responsible to the hospital board. Sometimes it was exciting and technically challenging, and other times she just felt stuck between a rock and a hard place. But she loved it nevertheless. There was still a lot to do here, and she'd always been up for a challenge.

She looked at a pile of employment contracts and a thick file regarding a sexual harassment complaint against a catering manager, all ready for her review. Bedtime reading. Geez, bedtimes had never been such fun.

And why, oh, why did an image of a naked Matteo suddenly flit into her head at the mention of bedtimes? It was impossible these days to think of anything without him straying into her thoughts.

She was not going to go to the pub. She was going to stay here and work. Neither was she going to indulge any fantasies about him touching her or kissing her or undressing her in a lift…

which was her most recent one…or perhaps something in the on-call room. She'd heard many a tale about that kind of thing happening in hospitals. But, no—it was all out of bounds.

When she eventually looked up again she realised her assistant was watching her while dragging on a coat. 'Yes, Becca?'

'I don't know where your head was right then, but it wasn't here. Maggie's coming in on Monday at two, Leslie will come straight after her shift on Tuesday at three-thirty.' Becca smiled. 'So, you never did tell me why you came back from Theatre so early. Weren't you supposed to be with Dr Delicious all afternoon, you lucky thing?'

Oh. That. The hospital grapevine was alive and kicking and the news was bound to spread fast. She might as well front up to it, take the ribbing and move on. 'You have to promise not to tell a soul. Or laugh. Or anything, at any point.'

With a very serious look on her face Becca drew a cross over her chest. 'My word is my honour.'

'I fainted.'

Becca bit her lips together to hold in a laugh. 'Aha. Hmm. Okay. Understandable.'

'Really? You think? Honestly?' Ivy breathed out

a sigh of relief. It seemed the legal personnel had the same approach to bodies as she did. Preferring to look at them from the outside rather than the inside. 'I can't tell you how much better that makes me feel. I was standing up for such a long time and it was very hot in there.'

'Well, he definitely makes me all hot and bothered too.'

'What?' She might have known Becca's answer would be hormone-related. 'Oh, for goodness' sake, I didn't faint because of him, I fainted because the air-conditioning was broken and all my blood was in my feet and, well, I...don't like seeing inside bodies much. Mr Finelli is just a man. He's nothing special. No need to get all giddy.'

'Tell that to your face, Ivy. It's all red and blotchy.'

Ivy threw her assistant a smile. 'You know, I preferred you when you were meek and polite.'

'Sorry. Overstepping a little?'

'Yes. Kind of.' But, truly, Ivy needed some people on her side. After the stuffy atmosphere in the board meetings and the heavy, long hours, which she really deep down didn't mind, sometimes it was nice to have a little girl time. Usually by the time she got home after a long day her flatmate had either gone to bed or had hit the town with her boyfriend. They had a great flatmate arrangement, it worked well and they didn't get under each other's feet, probably because they rarely spent more than an hour a week together. Which meant that Ivy would find herself alone most evenings. Which was fine, given she had so much work to keep her occupied, but sometimes… 'Are you heading off now? Have a good weekend.'

Becca shook her head. 'Actually, I'm heading over to the pub. Everyone goes there on a Friday night. It's—'

As her heart fell Ivy interrupted, 'Oh, you too? Let me guess, tradition, right?'

'Tradition. Yes, most of the admin and support staff go—in fact, a lot of the hospital workers go. It's always good fun and there's karaoke later.'

'All the more reason for me to stay here, then.' Shuffling bits of paper on a Friday night, looking across the road at the lights in the pub. Listening to the laughter. God, she could have her own pity party right here.

Becca frowned right back. 'It's fun. Really. You should come. You don't have to sing.'

It wasn't the singing. It was the company. Certain company that she didn't want to face again today. 'No can do. I'm busy.'

'It'll wait. Turn your computer off.' With a dramatic flourish Becca stepped forward, stacked the files on the desk into a large pile and handed them over. She grinned, with no hint of apology. 'I know…overstepping again, but it's Friday. Take your folders home and read all weekend if you like, but tonight you're coming for a drink. We never did get to celebrate your arrival here. And it's about time we did. I can't tell you what a breath of fresh air you've been in here.'

'But…I… Wait…' To refuse would be rude. But to tell the truth would be embarrassing and refute what she'd just said about Matteo being nothing special. Because, really, he was a teensy bit set apart from other men she'd dated in her dim and distant past. He was attentive and could be gentle and funny in a macho kind of way. Plus, he made her heart skip just a bit. And she was intrigued by him, by a man who could hold her attention longer than any other had. And by that body, which had her pulse racing at the strangest and most inappropriate moments.

Which was exactly why she had no intention of stepping over the threshold of that pub door.

'Really. No. I can't. I'm just going to head right on home.'

'Seriously, you've got this far, don't be embarrassed. You'll be fine, honestly. I bet it happens all the time anyway. People faint, get over it. Come on.' Becca tugged on Ivy's arm as she had been doing almost every step through the hospital corridors in an attempt to bring her down here to the pub, despite every excuse Ivy could think of. In the end she'd had to give in because, it appeared, no one was listening. 'Last one at the bar buys the round.'

'Fine. Just give me a moment.' Ivy watched her assistant's back disappear into the pub and took a deep breath. If she didn't look at him she'd be fine. He'd be in the middle of a group, she'd shimmy past out of eye contact and hide in a dark corner with the rest of the admin staff. *No problemo.*

Taking another breath, she pushed the heavy door open and stepped in. The noise was bearable, people sat in groups and she could make out some familiar faces in the far corner, but as the door swung closed behind her everyone stopped what they were doing and stared at her.

Huh-huh. This was her idea of hell. Even though no one spoke she could almost read their thoughts. *She's the one who fainted. Top lawyer who's deep-down weak.*

But at least Matteo was nowhere to be seen.

At the bar Becca was talking to the barman, and beckoned Ivy over. 'Seeing as you're paying, I'm having the biggest cocktail they do. A jug of Cancun margarita, I think. What would you like, Ivy?'

'A glass of wine, please. Red.' *Make it a big one.*

'They do a nice merlot. Oh, look...' Becca pointed across to the admin crowd, who were grinning and waving back. 'Everyone's so pleased to see you.'

'Or they're laughing at me.'

'So, Miss Ivy Leigh, you decided to brave it out after all?' *Great.* Matteo's voice behind her thrilled down her spine. She couldn't see him but every tiny hair on her body was standing to attention in some sort of annoying hormonal salute to his arrival. Maybe the admin crowd hadn't been waving at her at all, maybe they'd all been giggling and flirting and fluttering their eyelashes at him.

As she turned she controlled her breathing. She would not be impressed. She would not be impressed. She would not… *Wow*. Every time she looked at him his eyes pierced her—so dark and intense. And right now they were sparkling with mischief. The shadows and dips of his cheekbones seemed more acute today and he certainly rocked the swarthy tall, dark and handsome cliché. In a collared black shirt that showed off his broad chest and snug jeans that hugged his legs he looked dangerous and sinful and so out of her league. Not that she had a league or even wanted to be in one. But, it was safe to say, if she did, he would be stratospherically out of it.

'Good evening, Mr Finelli. Yes, I'm here. My assistant insisted and it looks like the whole hospital is here too, so that's good, I'll get the humiliation over and done with in one clean swoop. I'm just showing my face, having a quick drink and then…' She lifted her overloaded workbag, the zipper almost splitting with the contents. 'Work.'

'Ah, yes. It never stops.' Shoving a hand in his pocket, he pulled out a wad of notes and gave them to the barman. 'I'll get these.'

Becca grinned her starstruck thanks and went

to join the group in the far corner. *Double great. Thanks a bunch. Leave me here with him, why don't you? Traitor.* Ivy picked up her glass and nodded to him. 'Thanks. I owe you one.' Then she took a step towards her crowd.

'Not so fast.'

'Sorry?' Ignoring the flustered feeling in her chest, she turned back to him, wondering what the Italian for cold shoulder was. Because that was what she intended on giving him. *Freddo shouldero, matey.* 'I'm on my way over to Becca...'

But he didn't take the hint. Instead, he smiled. For a fleeting moment it was almost genuine. 'How are you feeling, Ivy? No ill effects? No more fainting episodes?'

'I'm fine, thanks. Absolutely hunky dory. I'll see you...Thursday? For my workshop?' *Round two.*

'Again with this.' His voice was grim, but his smile was infectious as he took her arm and gently steered her away from the busy bar to a quieter corner. And, to her chagrin, she went with him. Was it her imagination or could she feel everyone's eyes on her back? 'We're away from work now on neutral ground, and it's the weekend. People just want to relax and have a good evening, me included. How about we drop our guard a little?'

This could be interesting. 'This is where you lull me into a false sense of security then you pounce, right?'

He shrugged. 'I don't need to do that. We could just have a conversation and see where we get to?'

Nancy squeezed past them to get to the bathrooms. 'Hey, Ivy. How are you feeling? Okay? Is Matteo giving you some tips?' She winked. 'He's very good.'

Ivy looked at the curve of his mouth and imagined a million things he'd be good at. Then ignored the flare of heat circling in her gut. 'I'll bet he is.'

'With fainting cures, that is…'

'Obviously.'

As Nancy disappeared into the bathroom Ivy put her bag on the floor, took a long drink and felt the warmth of the wine suffuse her throat. 'She's a stirrer.'

'She's a joker, but she has a good point.' Matteo's smile hadn't dropped. 'How on earth are we going to get you ready to face the scalpel again next week?'

Aha. Plan A. 'I'll be fine. I was going to start by watching a few videos online. Type "kidney transplant" into a search engine and there are hundreds of operations right there to pick from. You get a bird's-eye view, too, and commentary. It's almost as if you're actually there in the room, without all the smells or noises or...' *Without you*, she thought, all large and looming and stealing her breath. So it would be videos all the way until she was inured to the gore, with the sound turned to mute and a decent bottle of wine for Dutch courage. Anything not to lose face again next week.

'Ah, yes. The joys of the web. Amazing what you can find.' His smile glittered teasingly.

She ignored that, too, knowing damned well he was referring to his glorious backside. Which she did not want to see. Or think about. At all. 'Like I told you, some people do actually put useful things up there. It can be very educational.'

'And you are not at work now, so you don't need to give me the chat.' He emphasised *chat* with a sarcastic twitch of his fingers. 'Enjoy whatever you find on the internet...but make sure you take your hands away from your face first. And that you're sitting…no, lying down. You'll have less far to fall.'

'Ha-ha. You really are enjoying this.'

'What's not to like?' he said, in a voice filled with smugness, like the cat that had got the grappa-laced cream. 'But I'm glad you want to come back and see the wager through. You have strength. You have this hard outer shell, but underneath there is a softer side to you. A side you don't always want other people to see.'

That touched a raw nerve. She was only protecting herself, something she'd learnt to do because of experiences with men like him. She'd already lost enough to a selfish, inadequate man who'd wanted to play God, so she intended to keep herself whole and had no desire to fall prey to any guy's wishes. Plus, she'd seen her mother curl up in a ball and weep over someone who she'd given a part of herself to. Watched her crumble until she'd thought she couldn't live without him, couldn't put one step in front of another. Couldn't function. Ivy had no intention of crumbling. 'Don't we all keep a side of us private? I imagine there's more to you than what you show, too, Matteo. It's just how we project ourselves to the world, that's all. We don't have to show all our sides to everyone.'

He looked at her for a moment, his eyebrows raised, then shook his head, clearly perplexed. 'I am me. This is it.'

'Sure it is.' All annoying and smug and pro-found Italian with raw sex appeal and, she decided, probably not a lot of substance.

He shrugged as if he was reading her mind and he didn't give a jot what she thought. He probably didn't. 'Okay, whatever you think. You have your mind made up, I don't intend wasting my time trying to convince you otherwise. But, seriously, take a few small steps. Watch a video or two and concentrate on your body's response. Make sure you even out your breathing. Make sure it's deep and slow and regular, not jumpy, like it is right now.'

Ivy took a long slow breath in, felt a thump of palpitation in her chest as she willed her heart to slow. 'My breathing is fine.'

'Really? Could have fooled me. Because right now I'd say you were about to hyperventilate.' He reached a hand to her earlobe and checked out her silver hoop earring, ran a finger across the sensitive part of her neck. 'See. When I do that...up it goes. You need to be aware of that.'

Hello, I am very aware. Too aware. Her heart jittered, her hand started to shake again as she rubbed the spot he'd touched. 'I'll bear that in mind.' And, for the record, if she was to have a *thing* with anyone, it wouldn't be with a sexed-up macho surgeon. She would choose someone interested in the kind of things she liked, art, literature, someone with class and sophistication.

Not just a nice ass. And nice hands. And a devastating smile.

The smile spoke. 'And relax. Know your body well enough that you can identify signs of tension and consciously relax. Or, another method if you start to feel light-headed, tense your arms and legs and get the blood flowing well. Wiggle your toes to make sure your venous return is sufficient.'

'Yup. Thanks.'

'And why not just start with watching someone take blood first...move on up to renal transplants in a day or so? You don't want to run before you walk. Yes?'

'No. Yes. Whatever. Thanks for the pep talk.' She tried, but failed, to keep the sarcasm out of her voice. 'You trained in psychology as well as medicine?'

'No.' His eyebrows rose. 'But I had to get back into that theatre on day two somehow.'

'Oh. You were serious earlier about being sick in the OR? I thought you were just saying that to make me feel better.' Something really had rattled the great Dr Delicious once upon a time? 'And even after that you went on and trained to be a surgeon? Why? Why didn't you go into something less gory if it made you throw up?'

'Because that wasn't my dream. My dream was to be a renal surgeon. I don't like to do second best.'

She didn't doubt that or that he'd fight tooth and nail for what he wanted. He was the kind of guy who always got what he wanted and was used to snapping out orders—and having them followed. 'Why renal surgery? Why not orthopaedics or plastics, or something else?'

He took a drink from his beer bottle and for a moment looked pensive. 'My sister needed a kidney when she was eleven. She got one, in the end, although it took some time. And I could see the immediate change in her. I got my little sister back, with no pain and a future and so much energy. It was like a miracle. They saved her life. It seemed such a fabulous thing to do that I set my heart on it.'

Again with the surprise. The man could do serious and personal. This was the side of him she'd thought he hid. But he'd been right—he was upfront and honest. In an irritatingly candid way. Maybe she just hadn't asked him the right questions.

And maybe she'd be better joining Becca right now. But hell if her feet didn't root themselves to the spot. 'Knowing how much demand there is for kidneys, I'd say she was very lucky. You have just the one sister?'

'No. Two sisters and three brothers. Yes, I know. It's a huge family by most standards. Even by Italian standards.'

'Wow. That must have been busy. Are they all like you? Your poor mother.'

'It was challenging, I think. In lots of ways it was hard for her.' His face almost dipped into serious, then he broke out into a smile. 'I am the oldest. I know what you're thinking, yes, they hated me. I'm bossy and organised and like being in charge. There isn't any insult you could call me that I haven't already been called.'

'I don't know, I'm sure I could think of a few.'

'Don't think too hard.' He took another drink. 'And you?'

'Me? No. Not many people have insulted me.' Actually, that was a lie, but it had been the pitying looks that had cut the deepest. No amount of physiotherapy and practice could cut the limp out completely. And with that thought the pain came shooting back up her leg, tripping across the scars. She instinctively shifted her weight, wishing she could change out of her work shoes into something more comfortable.

Matteo looked at her as if waiting for her to explain her sudden reverie. 'Ivy?'

'What?'

'I meant family,' he explained. 'You have brothers and sisters?'

'I'm an only child. I did have a stepbrother once, for a few years, and then there was a divorce—make that the second out of three—and they moved away.' She tilted her head a little to one side and found a smile to try to tell him she was fine with it. Still, it had been nice being part of something bigger. More than nice. And the fallout when Sam had left had been huge in so many ways, losing her stepbrother, Taylor, just one of them. *He's not your real brother, so stop whingeing. Imagine how I feel without my husband. How will I cope without him? How will I survive?* 'Largely it's been just me and my mum.' And a string of unsuccessful relationships.

'The doctor. And you didn't want to follow in her footsteps?' He grinned. 'Ah, no, of course, the fainting thing.'

'That and the fact that I hated hospitals for a long, long time.' And now she'd said too much. Looking for an out, she turned to look over at a commotion on the stage. 'What's happening over there?'

Again he looked at her with a quizzical expression. 'Why did you hate hospitals?'

'Look, I really should go.'

'I'm sorry, I asked you something you didn't want to answer.' His voice softened a little and she was startled and humbled by his honest, straightforward approach. Yes, he had asked. And, no, she didn't want to talk about it and see his pity and later his revulsion. But he continued chatting, undeterred, 'It's charity karaoke. The bar manager lets us have fifty percent of the proceeds if we get the crowd started. Every penny counts. We're fundraising for a new dialysis machine. We're always fundraising for a new dialysis machine. We will never have enough. We can only do so much to make our own miracles.' He picked up her bag and started to walk towards the stage. 'Come watch?'

'Er…will I have to sing?'

'If you want to help us raise money. And you said you did.'

Despite the endless irritation he instilled in her, the thought of spending more time with Matteo really appealed. Really, truly, and she knew it was nothing to do with helping him raise money. Panic took over from the pain in her foot. She could not want to spend more time with Matteo.

She shook her head. 'This wasn't what I had in mind. There's lots of other, bigger ways we can help. Besides, I've already made a fool of myself once today, thank you very much. Singing is definitely not going to help my cause of winning over the hearts and minds of the staff.' She checked her watch. 'I'm going home.'

'Matteo! Matteo!' A guy called over. 'Come

on, mate, stop chatting up the ladies and get that famous peach of a backside over here. We're starting.'

Matteo grimaced and raised a finger. 'Give me a minute, Steve.' Then he turned to her and she could have sworn his eyes flicked towards her feet and then back to her face. 'I'm never going to live that picture down. Now, how are you getting home? I'll walk you to the door and get you a cab. Or walk you to the car park.'

'It's fine. My bus stop's just over the road. I can walk across the pub on my own, and, believe me, it'll be a damned sight easier than walking in.'

'But you did it, and no one has said anything at all. Except me. And I have kept you all to myself.' Taking her glass from her hand, he gave her another warm smile. No—not warm. It was possessive. Hot. His hand brushed against hers and heat rippled through her. She tried to shake it off, but it stayed, curling into her, making her hot too. His voice was deeper when he spoke again, and it caressed her insides. 'Ivy, do you have to get back for the boyfriend? The husband?'

'No. I told you, I have work to do. I really do.' *Please, don't ask anything...more.* There was something about him that was different from other men, that connected with her on another level. Something about him… Her gaze slammed up against his, the warm tease now a molten heat. She wanted to…do so many things she'd promised herself not to do again. She didn't want to be beholden to a man. To fall too deeply in love with someone who would have a hold over her emotions and actions. She wanted to stay whole. To be herself, and so much more.

He shook his head. 'Okay. I know I'm going to regret this, but I'll let you go this time. Next week I might not be so lenient.' Was it her imagination or was he flirting again? She didn't know. Panic and heat rose in her gut. The heat overriding the panic, squashing it. No. This was not how she wanted to feel—she didn't want to lose control with him. Knew that if that happened she'd be on a spiral to disaster. She didn't need that in her life, not when she'd finally got where she'd wanted to be. His hand touched her arm. 'You're going to leave me to sing to these people, and I'll end up looking like a fool—as always—but it's worth it for the money. Don't work too hard, Ivy. Enjoy the videos.'

'I will.' *Another lie.* Breathing a huge sigh of relief, she pushed the door open and inhaled the late spring evening air. Thank God for that. What was happening to her insides she did not know, or want to even think about. But she knew she had to put some distance between her and Dr Delicious. Wrapping her coat around her, she began to walk towards the bus stop and realised…

My bag. Damn.

Without it her evening, her whole weekend, would be lost. Besides, those files held confidential information that she could not lose on any account.

Twirling back round towards the pub, she slammed hard into a wall of muscle. A dark collared shirt. Brooding eyes. A hand holding out her bag. 'Ivy.'

'Oh.' But now she was touching him she didn't want to let go. Should have but didn't. Underneath the soft linen of his shirt she could feel every nuance of muscle, every ripple of movement. And there, underneath her fingers, his heart beat strong and regular. Steady. 'Matteo—'

'Hush.' The bag fell to the ground. Then he

placed his palm to the back of her neck, pulled her towards him, and pressed his lips against hers.

It took a moment to register that this was Matteo, this was a kiss—so unexpected, and yet everything that their conversations had been leading up to. His mouth was playful as he nipped across her bottom lip and she could feel his smile against her own. Then she stopped thinking altogether—because thinking would throw up too many barriers, and just for once in her life she wanted to be free, to take what she wanted instead of holding back. To open herself up to...*this*. He tasted exotic, of spice and man, and it set her gut on fire.

Wrapping his arm around her waist and drawing her closer, he set the tone, and took control. His tongue slipped into her mouth and danced a fierce dance with hers. She gripped his shirt, pressed her body against his, took everything he gave her and gave it right back to him. All the fighting and the humiliation and the anger and the deep sexual need she'd experienced since she'd crossed paths with him was in that kiss. So too was a longing and heat that she'd never experienced before.

This was bad.

This was good.

This was the biggest mistake she'd ever made. As reality seeped into her brain she stopped. Fighting for breath, she pulled away. 'My God, Matteo. What the hell was that for?'

'You looked like you needed kissing.' And he was all bravado and outward calm but she could see the slight tremor in his body as he inhaled a breath. So it had been an instinctive unthought-out action and had taken him by surprise too. 'And I was right, you did. Kissing suits you. You should do it more often. Look at you now—alive. Vibrant. No words.'

She daren't imagine how she looked, but that was the least of her problems. 'Well, that's not the way I do things. And now I'm going home.' *Don't even think of asking to come with me.*

'Okay. If you insist.' As he appeared to get used to the idea that smile was back on his mouth. A mouth she'd actually, really, truly just kissed, in the street like a…an out-of-control teenager.

Kissing Matteo! She swiped a hand across her lips to remove all trace of him. What the hell had she been thinking? He was all mouth and smug and… Oh, my God, he was good. And she couldn't find an inch of her body that didn't want to do it again—but her conscience, oh, dear, her conscience was very unhappy with such a strange and unexpected turn of events.

'My bag? Please.' She reached for it.

'Sure. Here you go. Sweet dreams, Ivy.' With that he handed her bag over, turned and disappeared back inside the pub, leaving her breathless and hot and shaking.

Sweet dreams? Not if they were going to be filled with him. *Please, no.* Thanks goodness her bag was stuffed to the gills with papers that would keep her occupied into the early hours, because somehow she was going to have to keep her mind on her work and not on a peachy backside, startling eyes and smug mouth.

Good luck with that.

CHAPTER FIVE

'SERIOUSLY, I HAVE to sit in a circle and discuss hypothetical scenarios? Really? When there are real ones happening two floors down in ER...and an empty OR across the hospital?' Matteo looked around at the other members of the group in disbelief. Two doctors, a ward clerk and a phlebotomist. They were okay with this?

'Okay, then.' Ivy was hovering around them, going from group to group checking on progress, a smile plastered to her face. A smile, he could see, that wasn't comfortable every time her eyes settled on him. 'Why don't you share with everyone what the specific problems are for your department? We could do a brainstorm and set something in motion. It could be a true test of the skills you're learning here on the course.'

Marjorie, the ward clerk from ward three, nodded in agreement, her gaze homing in on Matteo. 'Okay, big-shot bottom, tell us what you need.'

He smothered a grin. That photo had certainly been one way of getting attention, unwanted but nevertheless—people certainly knew him now. 'I need, in simple terms, a new dialysis machine, or funds to buy one.'

'Ball park?' Ivy again.

'Around thirty thousand.'

'That's a lot of calendars you'd have to sell, Mr Finelli. How about you approach a fund starter website? That would be a great place to start. Some people are seeing amazing results...' Ivy certainly got impassioned and enthusiastic about some things. 'Set up an account and get people to pledge money. Those kinds of forums work because it's a little more personal than just donating. You could have giveaways with each level of pledge—say, a plaque for a platinum sponsor. Plus a brochure and a personalised photograph or something...'

'We've already got a perfect picture for that, eh, Matteo?' It was Marjorie again. His backside had certainly gone viral.

Ivy rolled her eyes. 'That's enough about that picture, please. I am so over it. Really. As I've already explained to Mr Finelli, that's not the sort of image we want associated with St Carmen's—as we can clearly see it distracts us from our purpose. Still, great work. Brainstorming certainly helps.'

One of the other doctors chipped in, 'How about a charity run or a bike ride? A run might work better—around one of the parks? Hyde Park would be good. I know they allow a certain number of small events like that. Or Regent's? Or a skydive?'

Ivy beamed and shot an *I told you so* look at Matteo. 'All of these things can catch the public's eye—given enough warning, they would embrace it. We could get the message out via our usual social media outlets—contact radio stations directly, and get their followers to get involved—it's a chain reaction. A personal message in a public forum often gets huge hits and a better positive response. Something like *Want to fly high for St Carmen's? Charity fundraising skydiving event—have fun and do some good! DM us back for details…* Or something. That's off the top of my head, and you'd need to do it in conjunction with marketing.'

Matteo nodded, impressed with the enthusiasm,

although daunted by the amount of time it would need to do all this. 'It sounds like a lot of work.'

'And we're not afraid of that.' Ivy tapped her marker pen against her mouth as she thought. 'It would be a team effort, anyway. Small amounts of time and energy spent efficiently, in the right ways.'

He preferred it, he mused to himself, when that mouth was not talking. When it was kissing him. Who would have thought that was how the evening would pan out? It had been a surprise even to him. More so, the way she'd kissed him back with such hunger had stoked a fierce heat inside him, one that had him wanting more from her in a way that he hadn't wanted someone in a very long time.

Which was warning enough. No more kissing.

The afternoon crawled along and eventually the workshops came to a close, and he wasn't sure whether it was such a coincidence that he was, once again, the last person to be leaving the room. His feet seemed to have started a revolution and were taking their time in walking towards the door.

'Mr Finelli. May I, please, have a word?' She

sounded like a schoolteacher. Which made him grin to himself. That kiss had shaken her. And it had probably been wrong of him to have done it—but, *Dio mio,* she had looked so uptight and uncomfortable and after the kiss it had been like looking at a different woman. Her hair had become messed a little and her lips had swollen, her cheeks pink, but her eyes—man, her eyes had been alive. That intense green flecked with gold, and sparkling. Just sparkling.

Despite that, he knew bone deep that it had been a crazy thing to do. He had no business kissing Miss Poison Ivy. They were poles apart in everything, not least that he was a one-night-stand man and she looked, as far as he could see, like a one-man-only woman. No—it wasn't going to happen again.

He turned, but made sure he stayed where he was at the door—all the better to make a quick exit before any more kissing happened. 'Sure. What can I do for you?'

'Nothing. That's exactly it. I don't want you to do anything else. Ever.' She walked towards him, her mouth fixed and determined. Her gait, as al-

ways, just the tiniest bit off balance. 'No touching. No kissing. Nothing.'

'The kiss? You want to talk about it? I thought
you would almost burn up with the heat. It was
good, yes?' Just thinking about it again sent hot,
sharp need rippling through him.

She shook her head, holding her workbag against
her chest. 'That's not the point.'

'You say that a lot.'

'Say what?'

'"That's not the point."' He removed his hand
from the doorhandle and tried not to touch her.
'When you deny how you're feeling, or what
you're thinking, you close off a corner of yourself.' And he should learn a lesson from his own
words—but, hell, he'd learnt to close himself off
to attaching any kind of sentiment to a kiss. It
was just human nature. It was lust. It was natural
desire, that was all. This time he was in control
and calling the shots and, besides, he had no intention of taking it any further. He just couldn't.
'It is exactly *my* point. It is a simple answer, yes?
Or no? You liked the kiss?'

'Is not the poi— Oh...' she frowned and he
thought for a moment she would stamp her foot

in irritation, but instead she gave him a haughty smile. 'You are insufferable.'

'Hey, come on, I was there. I know that you liked it. Try to be honest, Ivy. Your eyes give you away anyway. You liked the kiss and you want to do it again, but you won't. You have a very strong resolve and kissing won't get you where you want to be. Is that right?'

'Yes. Absolutely.'

'But still you liked it.'

Now she looked like she was trying not to laugh, that pretty mouth curling at the edges, light in the green eyes. 'You are very annoying, Matteo. Okay. If I say yes, will you shut up?'

'Perhaps. Take a chance and see.' He raised his eyebrows and waited. And waited some more as the silence in the room became amplified and the lack of anyone else there became more and more obvious. They were alone and if kissing was on the agenda it could happen here. Now. And no one apart from them would ever know. He perched on the edge of one of the tables. 'And…?'

She glared at him, all humour and frustration and tight-lipped. And eventually she shook her head and tsked. 'God, will you never give up? I liked the kiss, okay?'

As he'd thought. 'Good. You said it and nothing bad happened, so it wasn't so hard to be honest and open, was it? I liked it too, but it wasn't a sensible move.'

'No. It wasn't.'

'And if we do it again?' What was it about her that made him so rash? He wanted to say things to her that he'd never said to anyone else. 'You will slap me with a sexual harassment complaint?'

'Oh, no. I wouldn't do that. I fully acknowledge my part in it.' The smile gave way to a frown. 'It is mighty tempting.'

Indeed it was. Achingly so. And a lesser man might well have tried it again. But Matteo knew the score, he had nothing but respect for her and would not step over a line that she drew. But that didn't mean he couldn't be friends with her, somehow.

Friends? What the hell? A debate began to rage in his head. A man could have female friends, couldn't he? But friends with the woman he'd locked horns with last week? With the woman who enraged and entranced him? He'd find being friends with her very hard indeed. It would have to be work colleagues or nothing. 'So, we won't do it again. But for a moment last week I had a glimpse of what you could be like. You let me see a tiny chink of who the real you is. And then, bam, it was gone, all hidden behind the designer suit and the frumpy blouse.'

Her voice rose as she looked down at her top. 'It is not frumpy. It was exclusive—'

'And you are always so antagonistic, always fighting. Why did you have to learn to be like that?' His chest tightened a little, because he knew damned well that no one was born like that, knew that slamming up defences and fighting your corner was a learnt response. He'd been through that and out the other side, learning to withhold his need to fight back. Because, in the end, all that did was make situations worse.

Except, of course, when it was to do with a mandatory training course. He'd keep on fighting against that.

'I didn't realise. Oh.' Two hot spots blossomed on her cheeks. 'Is that how I come across? Antagonistic?'

Her frown deepened and he immediately regretted what he'd said. 'Maybe only to me.'

'I'm ambitious, I want to do well,' she railed at him. 'And I've earned my stripes, so in certain situations I get to call the shots.'

'I understand.'

She glanced at him as she dragged the door open with her free hand and held it open, leaning against it. 'Do you? Really? You understand how hard it was for someone like me to have achieved what I have?'

'Someone like you? What does that mean?'

'Oh, nothing. Forget it.' With that she stalked out of the room, favouring her left foot as always, and walked down the corridor.

'No. Tell me.' He caught her arm. There was a dare in her, a level that he connected with that was fresh and new and challenging and he liked it. A lot. She had depth, layers. Layers he'd like to unwrap. So, what the hell, he was never one to flinch from a challenge. 'I want to know.'

Her shoulders hitched nonchalantly as she slowed to a halt, surprise lacing her eyes as she looked first at his hand on her arm and then at his face. She was hiding behind bravado that was flimsy and fragile.

'Let's just say I didn't exactly have the most conventional route to getting to where I am now. At times it was a struggle and I had to fight very hard, to push myself. I have high expectations and I expect everyone to have the same. Sadly, they don't. I don't like to call it fighting or antagonistic, I prefer determined. Gutsy. And damned hard work. But, whatever it is, I learnt that to get anywhere you have to be prepared to go further than anyone else. And you always have to do it on your own. Because, in the end, you're the only person you can rely on.'

So, somewhere along the line she had been hurt. He got that now. And a dark feral anger shook through him, the ferocity of it shocking him so much he took a step backwards. But he shook it off. Not his problem. Not his fight. He never allowed himself to get swept up in a woman's dramas.

So he was startled by his reaction, his need to fight on her behalf. To protect her. And by the rush of something that clutched at his chest as he saw the pain in her eyes, and the fight. He dropped his hand from her arm but followed her, picking up her pace. 'They certainly picked the right person for the job here, then. I love St Carmen's but they do need to be brought into the twenty-first century. You'll have a challenge on your hands to do that.'

Once again they found themselves at the lift and she pressed the button. No jab-jab-jab this time; she didn't appear to be in such a hurry to get away from him. 'At least we agree on something. For sure, they do. I don't know when the employee contracts were last brought into line with the most recent laws, or the sexual harassment policies, not to mention the complaints procedures, but it wasn't this side of the millennium. So it's a hard enough job as it is, without having to be sidetracked by some jumped-up surgeon's bottom.'

'Touché, Ivy. Touché.' He leaned forward and whispered, 'That's not Italian for "You can touch it," by the way.'

'Ha! In your dreams, Finelli.' She flung him a disdainful sideways glance and shook her head. But he could see, as she hit the lift call button again, that her hands had a tremor. She was all talk of ballsy and brave, but underneath she was bubbling and boiling. 'Now, you must have something more important to be doing?'

More important, undoubtedly, but not as interesting. 'Yes.'

She nodded, all businesslike, as a queue began to form behind them for the lift. 'So, I'll see you tomorrow morning.'

'On Ward Four. Seven-thirty. We'll meet there.'

'Be prepared, Finelli. I've been doing my homework.'

Prepared? Sure. He kept trying to be, but just when he thought he'd got everything under control Ivy Leigh knocked him backwards or sideways or just plain upside down.

As Ivy stepped onto Ward Four she was consumed by the memories, the smell, the rush-rush of the nurses as they bustled by. The fear. That was it, the place smelt of fear. And no doubt that had not been the intention of the interior designer who'd recently been appointed to cheer the place up. Sure, they'd done a great job with the bright primary-coloured walls and the jungle-animal theme.

But it still smelt of fear.

Or maybe that was just her impression. Surely it was, because the kids she could see were cheerful and smiling and the parents too. It was just her and her memories. Of learning to walk again. Of the pain. And the loss. Of not knowing who was going to turn up to take her home. If, indeed, she had a home to go to.

Brushing those memories away, she fixed on a smile and headed towards the huddle of medics standing around a bed. As she closed in on them she heard Matteo's voice, soft and soothing, chatting to a little boy who was wearing Spiderman pyjamas and sitting up in front of a giraffe mural, with more tubes coming out of him than she'd ever seen.

Matteo stroked the kid's blond hair back from his eyes. Eyes that were dark and sunken and ringed and skin that was tinged with the grey pallor of sickness. 'So, Joey, what's so special about Spiderman? I mean, he can jump a bit, right? But that's all.'

'*Fly*. He can fly, silly. And he saves everyone. The whole world.' The boy's face was animated as he spoke, but depleted of energy, like a deflated balloon. 'He's very cool.'

An anxious-looking woman, whom Ivy presumed was the boy's mother, sitting on the bed next to Joey, smiled and said, 'Like Matteo? He's going to give you a new kidney, so he's very cool, too.'

'I do not think I'm all that cool. But maybe I should get a vest saying *Kidney Man!* on it? And a cape? Will that help me fly too? I quite like that idea.' Matteo examined one of the tubes, then grinned, his face boyish but wise. 'But first we have to make you better. And I'm going to do that this morning. We're going to go along and see my friend Mo who's got special medicine that helps you to go to sleep, and when you wake up you'll be feeling a bit sleepy, but much better. And you'll have a new kidney that means you can stop all the dialysis and a lot of the medicine and then we'll just have to see you sometimes and not every week. And soon you'll be able to go back to school and not be tired. How d'you feel about that?'

The boy nodded sagely. 'Good. Will it hurt?'

'We'll give you special medicine, and if you have any bits that hurt we'll make them all better for you.' As if he sensed Ivy's presence, he glanced over and raised his eyebrows, beckoning her over. 'Hey, this lady works at the hospital. She's new and she's learning how we do things. Is it okay with you all if she watches the operation?'

'Yes. Hello.' The boy stuck out his hand in such an old-fashioned, too grown-up gesture that tears pricked Ivy's eyes. He should be out playing, running around with his friends, getting into mischief, not here in a bed, waiting for the gift of life.

She blinked the tears away—because what use were they to him?—and took his sweaty little hand in hers. She'd never had a broody bone in her body but, heck, she felt everything soften at the faith the boy put in Matteo, and his acceptance of everything. Such trust. And the injustice that someone so little and innocent would even have to go through this. But Matteo was handling it so perfectly Joey didn't appear concerned. 'Hey, Joey. How are you?'

'Okay.'

His mum interrupted, 'He was a bit nervous earlier, but he's fine now Super-Matteo is here, aren't you, Joey?'

Ivy knew exactly how all that felt. The sick feeling in the pit of your stomach, the panic, the fear of the general anaesthetic. The fear of not knowing if she was going to wake up again. The fear of a pain that was uncontrollable. *Run*, she wanted to say, Run! But before she knew what she was doing she stepped forward, her voice low but as friendly and reassuring as she could make it.

'It does feel a bit scary at first, doesn't it? I know, I really do. It's perfectly normal to feel like that, but you'll be fine. Honestly.' She hoped to God he would be. 'Matteo and his friends are really great and you'll be all fixed up.' *And I'll be in there, making damned sure it'll happen.*

And if anything cemented the rightness of her taking this job it was this. Right here. That she was in the perfect place and that she would do her best to make sure everything went exactly to plan, for Joey and kids like him. She couldn't do it for the whole city, or the country, or right the wrongs of the world, but she could do this, make a difference here to these lives. Of course she recognised that Matteo, and his colleagues, were not at all like the surgeon who had operated on her— that these guys were capable and competent and fully aware of their expertise and limitations. And that this child's life and future was in their hands.

She also knew, without a shadow of a doubt,

that Matteo would never take a needless risk. And that she would trust him wholeheartedly with her own child's life. And that recognition shuddered through her. She believed in him. Was swept up in the passion with which he attacked his job—and, to her chagrin, the humility too. He may have been the single most irritating man she'd ever met but she trusted him. To do his job properly, at least. Anything more than that was a step too far for her right now.

He was looking at her with a strange expression and she realised she'd given away more than she'd intended. 'Yes, thank you, Ivy. We'd better all get along now. You want to bring anything with you, Joey? A special bear? Teddy?'

'Can Spidey come?' The boy held up a plastic miniature of the superhero, which Matteo took and stuffed into the boy's pyjama pocket. 'Absolutely. Where would we be without him?'

And with that he gave them all a nod, his gaze lingering on her for just a little longer than she felt comfortable with.

Game on.

CHAPTER SIX

SEVEN HOURS AND two operations later Ivy was definitely feeling the effects of standing and tensing and standing and tensing. Trying to stop herself from swaying, she shifted from one foot to the other, ignoring the sharp pain that shivered up her leg, and was so very grateful that she hadn't fallen over or fainted or shown herself up in any way. In fact, she was feeling pretty proud of herself.

At the operating table Matteo was deep in conversation with the medical students, showing them the difference between a renal vein and an adrenal one. She knew that herself, having studied it ad infinitum on the internet—firstly through her fingers and with noise-cancelling headphones. Then, as her confidence had grown and she'd remained upright, with more and more ease. Still not exactly comfortable, but less at risk of falling over. The good thing was that she knew what to expect, what was going to happen, and so knew when to look away or sing a little song in her head to mask the commentary.

Watching him work, she had a full flush of something like nerves, which she knew was all part of the attraction she now admitted she felt for him. And it was rash and stupid and she just wanted it to go and leave her in peace. Because before she'd ever laid eyes on that spectacular pair of buttocks she'd been quite happy. Okay, so maybe she'd been feeling a little like she was missing out on something in her life. But not enough that she'd been bothered to care. Work had been too all-consuming and she'd liked it that way.

But now? Now she wanted to put her hands on him again. To feel that chest fall and rise under her fingertips. To feel his lips pressed against hers.

His voice floated over to her as she focused on the floor and controlled her breathing. 'Yes... thanks for the help, guys. Great job. Now we can go and talk to the boy's parents with an update. Then off to the Dragon for Friday night drinks,' he was saying. 'Not too late for me today as I have to prepare for tomorrow. It's going to be an incredible game. You just wait, we'll give your team a good thrashing.'

'Can't believe you got tickets for Twickenham,' someone answered him. 'How much did you pay for them?'

Matteo laughed. 'I sold my soul. But it will be worth it. This time tomorrow we'll be two tries up, three if we stick to the game plan. Go, Italia! Okay, everyone, let's go.'

So they were finished for the day. Just fine. The OR staff bustled around her as Matteo flicked his gloves into the bin. 'Congratulations, Ivy, you have mastered the art of watching an operation.'

She smiled—not wanting to admit that she'd spent the better part of the time not looking where everyone else had been looking. She knew the floor intimately. 'Well, it hardly warrants congratulations, but I'm feeling pretty elated for the patient and his family after such a long wait and worry. How long will it take Joey to feel better?'

'Almost immediately. He'll be a little groggy, but the cadaver kidney is working—clearly, we need to keep a very close eye on it—but the magic works straight away.' Taking her by the shoulders, he steered her out of the OR and pointed towards a door. 'I need to talk to the parents and my covering on-call staff…I'm not rostered on this weekend but I trust them completely,' he explained. 'Go sit down in there and wait for me. I'll be in shortly to debrief.'

'I should really get back to my desk. I've got an important case coming up next week that I really need to do some work on.'

His eyes darkened as he shook his head. 'And you can work all through the night and every hour of the weekend once you leave here. But, Ivy, it's been a long day. Just go in there and sit for a few minutes. You are allowed to rest. In fact, I insist and I'm the doctor. This is my domain and I call the shots. Go. I'll be in soon.'

'Okay. Okay.' To be honest, she was feeling just a little too exhausted to argue. God only knew how he felt after concentrating so hard for so long, and now he had to pull on a smiling face and meet anxious parents. It had been an emotional day, and a seemingly endless one. 'You can have two whole minutes, but then I do need to go. Cases don't get won by sitting around, doing nothing.' She started to walk towards the door and her heart lifted at the promise of a seat, but she couldn't resist adding, 'But…for the record…'

His eyes flashed with something as he turned back to her. 'Yes?'

'You did really well.'

'I know.' His shoulders relaxed and he laughed. 'Praise from you? Wow, what can I say?' He patted his heart and with a sarcastic grin said, 'It means so much.'

'It should. I don't give it lightly.'

She slipped into the staffroom, slumped onto the sofa and kicked her shoes off. *Wow.* That felt good. Rubbing her left foot with both hands, she massaged the gnarls and dips and scars and eventually managed to get the blood flowing properly, and gradually the numbness started to ease. What they'd achieved in there had been truly amazing. In Matteo's words, they'd given Joey a future. That was something to be proud of. But how could he do this, day in, day out? How could they all? It was exhilarating but so emotionally draining.

One thing she knew—he'd been right when he'd suggested she live a little in his world. Now she felt she understood that it was intense and necessary and so, so important.

But so was hers. Behind-the-scenes stuff that

kept them all focused and kept everyone away from harm. They both had their roles to play.

But now…exhaustion dropped over her as she laid her head back and closed her eyes, just for a moment…

'Hey, Ivy.'

Was it a dream? A dark, soothing voice that worked magic over her skin. 'Ivy?'

Not a dream. Actually, here in person. Better than a dream. Or worse. She was here. He was here. Alone. And…hell, she was sleeping. That was so not the way she wanted people to see her, especially people like him.

Her eyelids shot open. He was close, kneeling on the floor next to her, an easy, teasing smile on his lips. 'Ivy? Are you okay?'

'Oh. Hello, Matteo. I…er…' She sat bolt upright, shoving her feet back into her shoes. Had he seen? 'Whoa, how long was I asleep for? I should be getting back to work.'

'No. Wait. Here.' He handed her a hospital-issue white porcelain cup with something that smelled like heaven in it. 'Drink this first. I smuggled it in from Enrico's so don't breathe a word to anyone.'

He'd brought her coffee? Staring at the cup, she grimaced. 'Did you put poison in?'

'Me? Poison the enemy? I wouldn't stoop so low. Besides, I get the feeling I've won this part of the battle.'

'I think I'm starting to see things a little from your point of view. But that doesn't mean I'm backing down or admitting a darned thing.' She took a sip and smiled, leaning her head back against the lumpy cushions. He'd brought her coffee? She didn't want to read anything into that. 'It's perfect. Thank you. How did you know what I liked? Guesswork?'

'When I described you to Enrico he said you always have the *caffe lungo. Americano... Grande...* whatever you all call it here. Strong and black.'

She didn't know what to say. 'Thank you. That's very nice of you.'

When he'd stormed into her office that first day she hadn't imagined he could be like this. She'd jumped to the conclusion that he was all mucho macho Italiano. And, yes, he was. But he was so much more than that. So much more that she was trying hard to resist. And he was making it harder by the minute.

'Ivy.' His eyes shot to her foot and back again, his voice softer. 'What happened?'

Oh, wow again. Straight to the point. 'That? Nothing much. It was all so long ago.'

'And yet still you try to hide it.' Slipping her shoe off, he examined her foot, holding it firmly when she tried to wriggle it away. 'An accident? A car? Crush injury or something?'

'A-ha. Or something.' What to say? She took a breath and thought, struggled for a moment. This was too personal, she never spoke of it, never referenced it—had tried to put that experience to the back of her mind—but even so, it fuelled her job every day. Would it matter if she told him? Was that opening up too much of herself?

Yes. 'Look, it's not important. Thanks for an awesome day. I'll get going now.'

His hand closed over her foot. It was warm. It was safe. The safest she'd felt for a long time. 'I'm not going to let you walk out of here until I know what caused this. I know that's hard for you. I know you don't understand the need to be open. But it will be fine to talk of it. It will help. Maybe. I want to know. For you.'

For you. God, what did that mean? But trying not to talk about it would make it seem like an even bigger issue—and, really, she wanted to downplay it.

'I…er…' She didn't know where to start, so she just started at the beginning. 'I was four. My step-dad was new to us, not married to my mum yet, in fact they'd not long met, and he was trying to show off—to *bond*. He had me by the feet and was swinging me round and round and at first I was enjoying it. But his grip was so, so tight and I was going too fast and too high and no matter what I said he just kept on doing it to impress my mum. I started to panic and wriggled out of his grip. Hit the floor. Broke my ankle.'

'Ouch.'

'Yep. Mum didn't believe it hurt as badly as it did so I tried to walk on it. A few days later it was just so swollen and painful I talked her into taking me to the hospital. Turned out it was bro-ken in a couple of places and had started to heal badly. The orthopaedic surgeon was new and… well, let's say he wasn't in the right head space to be working. He attached an external metal frame to fix it—but he didn't do it properly. The upshot was I ended up with a badly deformed foot and twelve more surgeries to try to fix it.'

'When you say not in the right head space...?'

The all-too-familiar anger rippled through her. 'Drunk. On whisky and power.'

'Oh.' He started to stroke over the scars that snaked round her foot, her ankle, her calf, the knobbly, mottled skin more sensitive to his touch. And again she tried to pull away. How many men had flinched at the sight of it? How many had laughed at her? How long had she endured the teasing at school and beyond? The revulsion? His eyes widened. 'That's a real shame. I'm so sorry.'

'Don't be. It's in the past.'

He let her foot down then settled himself on the other end of the couch. Lifted her foot again and continued to stroke it as if it was the most normal thing he'd ever done. He smelt of dark brown Betadine, that distinctive hospital smell, but overlaced with his own particular scent of spice and pure raw man. 'But you are still affected by it, Ivy, I can see.'

'Plenty of people have worse than this, you only have to spend a day in this hospital to see that. It doesn't hurt much.' Actually, it did. Not a day or an hour went by without pain, but talking about it made it worse. What had hurt much more had been the reaction from everyone else. *Cripple. Ugly. Time-waster.* Her own mother hadn't been bothered enough to listen, to care, to fight.

'But that's why you're here, doing this job.'

'Yes.' She twisted round and leant back on the arm of the sofa to get comfortable. As if having a man like Matteo touching her skin would ever be a comfortable experience. It was terrifying. It was lovely. 'Sure, that's my calling. Righting the wrongs. Capturing the evildoers and taking them to task. Saving the world. Maybe I should get a cape too. Super-Lawyer.'

'Sure, you'd look cute in Lycra. We could be a dynamic duo. But now I understand a lot more about you.' He paused, waited until the smile had faded. 'And he apologised, this man?'

'The surgeon? Never. But he was eventually struck off after he got caught doing a similar thing—maybe six years later. Turns out he was a serial drunk and had hurt a lot of people over the years.'

'And the man who was swinging you round and

round?' His face darkened. 'You went through too much because of him.'

She thought about how much to say. Did it matter? Was she breaking any of her own cardinal rules by just talking to Matteo? It was only words. She could do words easily. She just didn't have such a great handle on emotions. Especially not these new ones—desire, lust, need.

'My mum married him. They all said it was my fault for wriggling while he was swinging me. Said he thought my screams were because I was having fun, not because I was frightened. And Mum was so bowled over by him she believed anything he said. She wasn't interested in my version of events, or in seeking any recompense from the surgeon, or to try make sure he didn't maim anyone else's kid.' It was all too much trouble.

'So that's why you distrust people too. Ah, you are textbook.' He raised his eyebrows and wagged a finger at her.

She grabbed it and twisted slightly. 'Glad I'm so transparent when I thought I was much more complex.'

'And twelve more surgeries?'

She shrugged, trying at the same time to shrug

off the memory and the pain she'd endured time after time after time. And learning to walk. Over and over. 'Yep. Internal fixations, pins, plates. Infected wound debriding… You could say I was more of an in-patient than an out-patient for a lot of my growing up. It got to the point that I used to take myself to my out-patient appointments on the bus on my own.'

'As a child?'

'As a young girl. A teenager. Mum wasn't very good at the parenting details of being a mother. There were always too many other things for her to do…' Or, rather, men to pursue. Relationships to sort out. Dramas. Lots and lots of dramas. Unfortunately, not one of them had involved looking after the only child she'd ever had. 'It was just easier to do it on my own than try to rely on her. Although, obviously, she had to come to sign the consent forms for the surgeries, but she didn't tend to hang around much.'

It had always felt as if it had been just too much of a hassle for her. That her needs had been a hindrance to her mother's social life. Until, that was, every time her mother's life had imploded, and then she'd clung to Ivy the way she'd clung to her husbands—with the desperate, all-consuming need that they all learned to despise in the end. The need that Ivy had seen once too often in her friends—the need for a man that overwhelmed them.

So she'd vowed never to be like that. Ever. Never to let a man take over, to take so much of her that there was too little left. But she didn't feel in any danger of that happening with Dr Delicious here—she knew exactly the score with him. He was the kind of guy who didn't offer any promises, and that was just fine, because she didn't want any.

The stroking of his hands had become more intense, the sensation he instilled reaching more than just her leg. It was travelling through her, heating every part of her. He nodded. 'So this is why you're so independent and argumentative? Because you want justice. And because you need to be heard. Because your mum let you down.'

She thought about it, and, yes, he was probably right, but she didn't want him to know that. Like a lot of things, it was easier to shove them deep down than face them. 'I suppose you could say that my relationship with my mother is as broken as my foot.' In fact, the thought of even discussing anything other than the weather with her mum brought Ivy out in hives. As far as she was concerned, it was better to be on her own than risk her heart again. A girl could only take so much emotional fallout.

'Thanks for the psychology lecture. But I'm just who I am, Poison Ivy, who won't tolerate defective people thinking they're immune to the law or to recrimination. Or surgeons who think they're God. Or people who don't take me seriously. Okay, so I've learnt to be like this, but I'm not ashamed of it.'

'You are Ivy. Yes. And you are stronger for your experiences.'

'And do you know, I don't think I've ever really talked about them before.' Not in so much detail. So God only knew what the hell that meant. That she'd exposed her weakness, not only allowed him to see her scars but discussed them too.

Suddenly she felt a little vulnerable. She shrugged her foot from out of his hand and scuttled her feet under her bum as she sat up, inadvertently shuffling closer to him as she resettled herself. 'So, please, please, don't say anything to anyone, I don't really want this to be hospital gossip. Every surgeon's going to think I'm on some kind of witch hunt and I'm not at all. I just want to do my job to the best of my ability, and scuttling out dodgy surgeons is only a tiny part of it. The rest is to put systems in place to prevent these things happening again.'

He frowned. 'Of course. But the scarring and the injury are hardly something you should be ashamed of.'

'If you'd seen the cruel reaction of the kids I grew up with, and then the men I dated who wanted tabloid perfect, you wouldn't be saying that.'

'Then they are all idiots.'

Yes. Maybe they were. And so was she for being taken in by his words. By his touch. By the way he sounded so unlike every man she'd ever dated— his words like a salve to her wounds. By the little dimple in the cleft of his chin. And by that tiny frozen part of her that had started to thaw, just a little, leaving her open and vulnerable.

She did not want this. Did not have space in her life for this. And, really, she should have stood up and left, but she reached to him anyway, placed her hand over his. Because it seemed a perfectly natural thing to do. 'Thank you. That was a nice thing to say.'

'My pleasure.' His hand cupped her face and he looked at her with such intensity that her heart beat a wild staccato against her ribcage. 'So don't be so hard on yourself.'

He was just being kind in that Italian way of his. He was being gallant and it was so nice to actually be on the receiving end of something like that. Just for once in her life. And he was so close. Looking down with a heated gaze that stoked something deep inside her. Something that answered the question in his eyes.

Then, unable to stop herself, she lifted her face and pressed her lips to his.

What kind of madness was this? Matteo mused in a barely coherent thought process as his hands curled around her, dragging her onto his lap and returning the kiss like a starving man. He was jaded and cynical and not able to offer anything more than this.

Her fingers spiked his hair and she moaned his name, her voice tinged with that cute accent that was so different and refreshing and intriguing and haughty. She tasted delicious. Of risk and freedom and the melting of barriers. Of layers and depth and heat. And wetness.

Her tongue slipped into his mouth and meshed with his, dancing an age-old dance that fired an intense need within him. He pulled her against him, relishing her soft body against his, and then, unable to wait any longer, he slipped his hand underneath the scrub top to her bra. With one easy flick of his fingers he'd undone it and palmed a hand over warm silken flesh and the tight bud of a nipple.

At his touch she moaned again, wriggling her backside against his erection, slowly gyrating on his lap. She was driving him crazy. Wild with desire. That clever mouth that kissed as well as it shot out smart retorts. This achingly sexy body with the softest skin and the scars of a history that made his gut clench. And that drive deep within her that had elevated her from her experiences and made her so much more. He wanted to do anything to erase that hurt.

But wait.

Taking her in the staffroom? That was not his

plan. She was worth more than that, deserved more. What kind of madness indeed. But he wasn't thinking straight. It had been a long, hard day and she was just so irresistible. Such a bundle of contrasts, and so damned hot. And he did not know what any of it meant, what this need that drove him was about, that he dreamt about her. But he knew it was intense. That it was something he should be afraid of, yet at the same time he was intrigued and, *mio Dio*, he just couldn't keep away.

A vibrating whirr and a tinny sound had her jumping off him, swiping a hand across her mouth and straightening her top. She reached into her pocket, pulled out a phone and frowned. 'Oh. Er... strange? I should probably get this.'

'Sure.' It would give him time to calm down a little and get things into perspective. Actually, to man up and put a stop to this fooling around in a public place. *Said the guy with his ass hanging out over the internet.* The more he thought about that, the more he realised what a stupid prank it had been. But he wasn't about to admit that to Ivy.

She turned away from him, her shoulders rising up to her ears as she talked. 'Oh. Okay. I see. When? Where?'

A silence stretched as she listened. The longer she stood there the more her body tensed, her hand slowly moving up to her mouth. And, as if in harmony with her, Matteo's heart clutched too. Clearly there was a problem and it went deeper than a work issue.

'Of course,' she said finally, her voice weak and wobbly. 'I'll be there as soon as I can. Please, tell her to…I don't know… Tell her to hold on.'

As she slung the phone back into her pocket she turned to him, her face pale now, all traces of their passion erased. 'I have to go back to York. My mum's sick. She's had a heart attack…they think, they're running tests as we speak. Er… she's asking for me.'

'Of course. You must go.' But there was something about her hesitation that gave him pause too. After all, it hadn't sounded like she had the best relationship with her mother. And he knew how being angry and disillusioned with family could affect someone. 'You think that's the right thing to do?'

She raised her head enough to hold his gaze,

and in her darkened, hooded eyes he saw fear and sadness and determination. Her voice was calm. 'Just because she's a lousy mother, it doesn't mean I have to be a lousy daughter. If she needs me, I'll be there for her.'

'Of course, and you shall go. Do you need help organising things?'

'Oh. Well, I guess I need to either hire a car or get the train. Driving's crap on a Friday, but it means I'll be able to go see her straight away, and also pop home for things she might need. But I think the train might be quicker…but…I don't know…' She took a step forward, then back. Almost as if she didn't know how or where to start. For the first time since he'd met her she seemed totally out of her depth. Blindsided.

And he needed to step up.

Didn't want to—because that would make things infinitesimally more complicated. But it wasn't about him. Or this. It was about her and healing things with her *mamma*. 'I'll take you.'

'What? No. No. No, don't be silly. It's fine. I can drive. I just need…' she fished her phone out again '…to call a decent car hire place…or something.'

Wrapping his arms around her, he took the phone from her hands, gave her a hug that she clearly didn't know what to do with but accepted anyway. And he was probably doing this all wrong and sending the wrong message, but he couldn't stand here and watch her sink. She was too proud for that. 'You are upset. Look, you're shaking. You shouldn't drive. Let me take you?'

She shook her head vehemently. 'No, it's too much to ask anyone. This is my problem, not yours. Besides, it's a hell of a long way, a good four hours' drive on a Friday night—more, probably, the traffic's usually a nightmare. You can't do it there and back in one go, not after a long day. And don't you have plans for tomorrow? A rugby game you sold your soul to the devil for or something?'

He hugged her to him, as he would have any friend who was suffering, trying through his actions to say what he wasn't yet ready to say in words. Hell, he didn't know what he was trying to say.

'It's rugby. We will win. It will be over in eighty minutes. This is more important.' *You* are more important, was what he actually thought. The shock of that shuddered through him. He didn't know her. He didn't like her, goddamn. Okay. So he could probably admit to liking her when she wasn't being a prim lawyer chasing his ass. Literally.

She spun out of his arms, looking embarrassed and flustered and about as far from a prim lawyer as anyone could get. 'And what about Joey and your other patients? They need you here.'

'I told you, the on-call team is fabulous—the best in the city. In fact, Dave Marshall taught me everything I know about renal surgery. So they're all in the best hands. It is fine. Really. I'm not due at work until Monday as it is, and I'm only a phone call away.' And he should have heeded the warning bells again then, but he didn't. Should have remembered the last time he'd allowed a woman to invade his life and his heart—and then plundered it and smashed it into tiny pieces and thrown it into the trash. The betrayal. The double whammy of hurt.

But this was different. Ivy needed help and he could give it to her. What kind of a man did otherwise?

CHAPTER SEVEN

IT WAS LATE and dark when they arrived at the hospital, after a long journey where Ivy had felt herself withdraw into her worries. But Matteo had kept a constant stream of trivial conversation to dredge an occasional smile and for that she was grateful.

Now she knew he liked rugby more than football. That he preferred bottled beer to wine. That he'd had his wisdom teeth removed when he was twenty. Nothing deeper than that. But it had been enough. More than enough to keep her from going out of her mind with concern.

He pulled up outside the entrance, a hand on her knee as he spoke. 'I'll find a parking spot. You go in, I'll find you.'

'She'll be in the cardiac ward, I imagine. Or High Dependency or something…I'll ask at Reception. Perhaps I should text you?' She went for her phone in her bag. Did she have his number?

He put his hand on hers and gave her a smile that went bone deep. 'Ivy, I know my way around a hospital. I'll find you. Go.'

'Of course. Yes. Yes.' What was wrong with her? One stolen kiss and she'd been reduced to fluff. Her brain wasn't functioning. Maybe it was the worry about her mum…

After she watched him pull away she went to find her mother, feeling empty and bewildered, her own heart bruised and broken enough too. There was so much between them that needed to be said, that she wanted to fix but wanted to avoid at all costs.

The hospital corridors were silent as she walked to the reception desk, a grey-haired lady pointing her in the direction of Cardiac Care. Darkness outside the windows penetrated her heart. She'd been talking about her mum and then something bad had happened. What did that mean?

She didn't want to rail at her, to blame her for the crappy upbringing she'd had—it was too late for that. All Ivy had ever wanted was recognition that she was important in her mother's life. But, in the end, she supposed, it didn't matter a jot. Ivy's mother was important to her and if love only went one way, then so be it. It was too late for recriminations.

One of the nurses greeted her and showed her to her mother's bed with a stern warning to be quick and quiet.

'Ivy.' Her mum looked frail and old, lying on pale green sheets that leached colour from her cheeks. Tubes and wires stuck out from under the blanket, attached to a monitor that bleeped at reassuringly regular intervals. A tube piped oxygen into her nostrils, but she sucked in air too, pain etched across her features. 'Thank you for coming, I said not to bother you. I know you're busy—too busy to have to come all this way to see your old mum.'

'Mum, you've had a heart attack—since when was that not enough to bring me to see you?' Guilt ripped through Ivy, as she'd known it would. It was what happened every time she saw her mum—whatever Ivy had done it had never been enough to make her mother love her and she just didn't know how to make things better. She gave her a hug, which was always difficult, and this time it was hindered by the tubes. Movement made her mother's monitor beep, and consequently made

Ivy's heart pound—loudly—and so she quickly let go. The space between them seemed to stretch.

'How are you feeling?'

'Lousy.' Breathless and wheezing, her mum settled back down and the beeping stopped. 'I had… an angioplasty. They've cleared the occlusion… put in a stent…so I just need a short stay in here… then do some rehab…as an out-patient.'

It was fixable. Just faulty plumbing. Relief flooded through her as she held her mum's hand. But once again she felt very much like their roles had been reversed, that she was the one taking the care, being the parent. 'That's great news. I was…I was worried about you.'

'Thanks, love. I'm glad you came. You're all I've got now. Can you stay…you know, a while?'

Responsibility tugged Ivy in every direction. Her job, everything, could be put on hold. Couldn't it? She'd only been there a few weeks—but they'd understand. Wouldn't they? She had a nagging sensation that things weren't going to be easy, that she'd have to fight to take time off—time she hadn't yet earned. And she had that upcoming sexual harassment case that was so important for everyone involved. She needed to be in London all clued up for that.

And she needed to be here with her mum. Someone who had never been there for *her*. Maybe she could trust the case to a junior? Maybe she could teleconference with them all. Maybe, *surely*, they'd understand? What would happen if they didn't? She didn't want to contemplate that. She'd finally got her dream job, and now… She looked at her mum, frail and anxious. 'I'll stay here with you as long as you need, Mum.'

'I'd appreciate it. I don't have anyone else.'

'You have me.' Even though it had never seemed enough. 'Is there anything you need? Once they have you settled…'

'I've been thinking, Ivy. About everything… We need to talk. *I* need to…' Her mum's eyes drifted to a spot just behind Ivy and as her skin prickled in response to an external stimulus, also known as Dr Delicious, she turned. Her mum's voice suddenly sounded a lot more healthy. 'Who's this?'

'Oh. Yes. Mum, this is Matteo, my…' What the hell was he? Other than a giant pain in the backside and a damned fine kisser? And, okay, so he was wearing her down a little with his huge generosity of spirit and the four hours' of driving on a soggy spring evening through interminable traffic on a motorway that had been as clogged as her mother's arteries. He was also messing with her head. 'He's my colleague at St Carmen's. He drove me here.'

'All the way from London? Lucky you.'

'Yes, well…' She'd never introduced a man friend to her mother before. 'He's just helping me out.'

Ivy shot Matteo a look that she hoped would silence any other kind of response. Because it was late and she was frazzled, her mum was sick and this wasn't the time or place for explanations. *I met his bottom first, the rest came later, and I have no idea what any of it means.*

And, truth be told, I'm scared. Right now, of everything. Of you dying. Of him becoming too much to me. Of losing myself in either grief or love.

Of not being able to let go.

The nurse bustled over and fiddled with an IV line attached to a large bag of fluid. 'Hello, there. Look, I know you've come a long way and I hope you don't mind me saying this, but visiting hours finished a long time ago. I let you sit with her for a while but, really, she needs to get her rest and so do my other patients...'

'It's okay, Ivy. You go.' Her mum's eyes were already closed, but she squeezed Ivy's hand. A gesture that was the simplest and yet most pro-found thing Ivy had received from her mum in a very long time. Tears pricked her eyes.

'Of course. Yes. Of course. I'm so sorry. I'll be back tomorrow, Mum.'

'Good. Bring me some toiletries, will you? A nightgown. Make-up.'

'Make-up? What for?'

'Standards, darling.' Typical Mum. But it did make Ivy smile—she couldn't be at the far end of danger if she wanted to put on mascara.

'Let's go, Ivy.' Matteo touched her arm and he drew her away from the ward and out into the si-lent corridor of eternal half-night. That was how hospitals felt to her—places where reality hov-ered in the background, and time ticked slowly in an ethereal way.

It was good to have him there, despite the strange unbidden feelings he provoked. Emotions washed through her—elation that her mum wasn't going to die, sadness about the gulf between them, and then, interlaced with all of this, the comfort of being with Matteo. A comfort that pulsed with excitement and sexual attraction. Which seemed really inappropriate and out of place right now. But there it was. Maybe she just needed another human being to metaphorically cling to. There was, after all, a first time for everything.

He waited until they were outside before he spoke. 'So it's good news, then? She's going to be okay?'

A long breath escaped her lungs. 'Yes, it would seem so. She's had an MI and angioplasty and the outlook's good.'

'So why the sad face?'

She tried to find him a smile, because it was good news. 'I don't know… I'm really pleased she's okay. I just feel terrible for saying those awful things about her, for thinking bad things when she was so sick. She could have died and I'd never have forgiven myself.'

He stopped short and looked at her. 'Ivy, her only job was to love you. If she didn't do that then you're right to be angry at her.'

She got the feeling that he was talking from personal experience, that there was something that had happened to him. That he understood what she felt because he'd felt it too. 'Matteo, do you have a good relationship with your family? Were things okay when you were growing up?' It was so not her way to ask direct questions like this—to go deeper than she ever wanted to go herself—but maybe learning how other people coped with things could help.

And she'd quite like to feel she wasn't the only one around here who'd got issues.

At a time like this, in the dark, late at night, with worry hovering around the edges, maybe it was the best time to talk about these things. The things that really mattered.

He shrugged, sucking in the cool fresh northern air. 'My mum could only be described as wanting to love us all to death. She's your typical Italian mother—overfeeding, over-smothering and over-loving us.'

'And your father?'

He shrugged. Opening the car door, his demeanour changed, his voice took on a forced jolly tone. 'Now, we need to eat something half-decent that isn't wrapped in plastic packaging and sold for a fortune in a motorway service station, and you need to get some serious sleep. It has been a long day.'

'Matteo...' She wanted him to continue talking about his family. This was the guy who believed in openness and honesty. But only, it seemed, when he felt like it.

'No, Ivy. It's too late for talking. Now, show me the way to your house.'

The emotions didn't wane as she shakily put the key in the lock of her mum's central York Georgian townhouse. It had been a long time since she'd been here—too long. And that last time they'd argued—but that was nothing new. Ivy couldn't even remember what it had been about. It didn't matter, it could have been one of a zillion things, as there'd always been an undercurrent of dissatisfaction between them. But she did remember that she'd left in a storm. And now she was back because her mum had nearly died.

They were immediately greeted by the smell of coffee—that was one thing she had inherited from her mum, a love of decent coffee. Then the warm press of Hugo, the fat ginger cat, who purred as he rubbed himself against her legs, preventing a step forward or backwards.

'Hey, cat.' Matteo took a sidestep through the front door, carrying Ivy's suitcase, a small overnight bag of his own and two large brown paper carriers. He walked through to the kitchen, knowing exactly where to go as if he had homing radar, and plonked them all on the floor. Looking around at the modern granite surfaces and white cupboards in a house that was over two hundred years old, he smiled. 'Very English. Nice. My mum would be green with envy if she saw this place. She's been talking about having a new kitchen since I was born.'

It felt strange, having him here in her space—her old space. It wasn't as if it felt like home any more and yet it was filled with so many familiar things and smells that gave her strange sensations of hurt and loss and loneliness. She'd always envied her friends who'd had happy chaos at home, whereas hers had been all bound up with suffering of one kind or another.

'So what's your home like, Matteo?'

'I guess you'd call it quaint. Old. Small. Traditional. Stone walls, dark wooden cupboards, terracotta tiles, in a village where everyone knows everyone and everyone tries to outdo each other. That's why I like London, you don't have to live in each other's pockets.' He nodded to the bags. 'Okay, so I got what I could from the little super-market next to the hospital after I parked. It wasn't great, but it had the basics. I have some chicken breasts, pesto sauce and mozzarella cheese. A plastic bag of something the label refers to as salad but which appears to be just leaves. Olives. Bread. And red wine.'

'I thought you said you preferred beer.'

Not hiding his smile, he started to unpack the carriers. 'So you were listening? I thought you were nodding your head in time to the music as you stared out of the window at something no one else could see.'

'I was listening.' It wasn't a lie. She'd been half occupied with dreary thoughts, and half enthralled by the thought of being with him for the next few hours. Alone. 'Well, thank you. I like red wine.'

'I know.' He rustled in the cupboards and fished out a frying pan, some bowls, a chopping board, two glasses and a knife. Then he opened the wine, filled two glasses and handed her one, gently pushing her to sit at the breakfast bar. 'Drink this while I cook.'

She did as she was told, enjoying having someone to look after her for a change but simultaneously feeling a little ill at ease. 'Why are you being like this? So kind and helpful?'

Slicing the chicken, he threw it into the pan and tossed it around in garlic-infused oil, then emptied the leaves into a bowl. 'Because you looked like you needed a helping hand.'

She thought about that. With his explanation it all seemed so obvious and easy. It wasn't. 'You once said, too, that I looked like I *needed* kissing. Do you always presume things, Matteo? Make up your own reality to suit yourself?'

He stopped chopping for a moment, the knife held in mid-air. 'As you appear not to be able to express your wants and needs, but to repress them and create barriers instead, in some sort of stiff-upper-lip thing, I have to go by gut instinct. Women! You should say what you want. Be honest. Ask and we'll help. Hinting and hiding stuff just confuses us. Pretending to be okay when you're not doesn't help anyone in the end.

And definitely not men...' He pushed the olives towards her. 'We're easily confused.'

'Poor men.' She shot him a sympathetic grimace. 'How did you get so knowledgeable about women?'

'I have two sisters, remember? You learn a lot rubbing shoulders with them twenty-four hours a day.'

'And girlfriends?'

His forehead creased into a little frown and he paused, this time the hand in mid-air holding a bowl of olives. 'Of course. I'm a man. We have few desires, but some of them do involve having a woman around.'

Oh, yes, she could see that he was man, thank you very much. In dangerous proximity. And she had no idea why she was taking the conversation down this particular track. 'Anyone...serious... ever?'

'Not really...' He shook his head, eyes guarded. 'No. I'm an emotional Neanderthal, apparently. Selfish. Unfeeling. Because I like to put work first, because I devote myself to my patients.'

'Poor you.' She leaned forward and gave him a kiss. A gentle one, on the cheek.

He rubbed the spot her lips had touched. 'What was that for?'

Shrugging, she threw him a smile. 'You looked like you needed kissing.'

His eyebrows rose and he laughed, full and heartily. 'Round three to Miss Ivy.'

She hardly knew him—and yet there was something soul deep that attracted her to him, a peace and yet a disturbing excitement. It felt natural to talk to him, and the silences were comfortable. She couldn't remember having had that before with a man. She'd spent a lot of time in previous relationships trying to be perfect, to make up for her leg and her limp and her over-officious use of words, her weird sense of humour, trying to give a little of what she held so precious. In the end it had all been hugely disappointing and not worth the trouble.

But Matteo wasn't like that. He was fun to be around. Plus he was pretty damned useful in the kitchen. With a nice bum. Or maybe he was just Mr Too Good To Be True? She flashed him a smile. 'Round three? Are we battling again? Why, when you know you won't win?'

'I will win. Just wait and see.'

She took an olive and popped it into her mouth. Swallowed. Thought a little more about Matteo, who was stir-frying with gusto. 'I suspect this "not really" woman broke your heart?'

'No.'

'Come on.' She narrowed her eyes. 'I thought you were all about being honest and open.'

His frown stuck in place as he emptied the frying-pan contents onto a plate, which he pushed into the centre of the breakfast bar. With a swirl of salt and a crackle of black pepper he finished the presentation with flair. Then carved a few thick slices of fresh white bread and loaded them onto side plates with the mozzarella, handing one to Ivy. 'In truth, she broke my trust and that's worse.'

'Oh, yes. Indeed. I understand that.' So there had been someone significant. And why that knowledge made her heart beat a little faster she didn't want to know. The way the colour had drained from his face told her he'd been hurt badly. That deep down he kept some truths to himself.

He stuck his fork into a piece of chicken and nudged her to do the same. 'Come on. Eat. It's getting cold.'

She didn't miss the fact he'd changed the subject. Or that he hadn't said he was happily looking for The One. But, then again, neither was she.

For that matter, she wasn't looking for anything—fling or attachment, or the whole wedding catastrophe. She was looking for peace of mind and a lifetime doing her own bidding. Of reaching her full potential. Of being the person she was destined to be. Without a man in tow. Without giving anything up. Without losing any of herself.

But a little fun on the side might be nice.

That wine was going to her head. She pushed the bottle away from her. No more. 'I think I'll make a start on the washing up.'

'Let me. It's past midnight, you look exhausted. Go to bed.' He reached for her dirty plate and his hand brushed against hers. They both froze as the connection, the electricity between them, blazed again, bright. He frowned. 'Go. Go to bed, Ivy. I'll sleep down here on the sofa.'

'You don't need to, there's a spare room upstairs. I'll make it up for you—give me a couple of minutes. First door on the right.'

'Okay. If you want.'

What she wanted was for him to sleep in her bed. *My God.* She didn't?

She did. And to wake up to that gorgeous smile tomorrow. Preferably with all her current worries wiped clean and her sense of self intact. She wanted to sleep with him and to have no ramifications. No angsty emotions. To be freed up enough to trust him. To trust herself to not be like her mother.

Like that was going to happen.

'Matteo...' She didn't know what she wanted to say. Well, actually, she did, but she didn't know *how* to say it. Or what saying it would mean for both of them. So she chickened out. 'Thank you. For everything. You've been very sweet.'

'My pleasure.' He ran his thumb down her cheek, his eyes kind and startling and misted. She caught his gaze and they stood for a few moments just looking at each other. So much was being unsaid, so many needs and wants. Eventually he dragged his gaze away. 'Now go.'

'But—'

'Please.' He must have known what she was going to ask, knew what she was thinking of offering him—it was written in her eyes, in her body language, in every word, in every gesture. But instead of reaching for her he shook his head. 'Ivy, it's late and it's been an emotional day. First the surgery, then your mum. Don't let's get things mixed up. Don't do something you'd regret.'

I wouldn't regret it.

But, then again, he was probably right. She had enough problems already without adding him to the list.

CHAPTER EIGHT

SOMETHING WARM AND heavy and very noisy pressed against Matteo's chest. Gingerly opening one eye, he came nose to nose with a fat cat that was purring so loudly it sounded like a dentist's drill. 'Hugo? *Ma, che sei grullo.* Eh? You *are* joking? A beautiful woman next door and this is the only offer of bedtime action that I get?'

Matteo wiggled and jiggled his torso but the cat didn't move. He just stretched a lazy leg, gave it a lick, then resumed the loud drill noise. 'Go, cat. Go.'

Purr. Purr. Another lazy lick.

'Okay. Stay there. See if I care. Because I don't.' It was six-thirteen in the morning. He was in bed with a cat. At Ivy's house. She, however, was sleeping elsewhere. That cross mouth and taut, hot body under covers in another room in a house that felt like it was the furthest thing from a home that he'd ever known. There were few pictures on the walls, nothing to say that a family lived here. Or a proud mother. Nothing like the chaos of his home, where you couldn't move for people and things. And the comparison made his heart ache for Ivy and what she hadn't had, growing up.

It had been a mistake to come here, that he knew with certainty.

He'd been so close last night to suggesting things that would have taken them way beyond this strange relationship they had right now. But just because he'd kept silent didn't mean he was happy about it. Or that he wanted her any less. But he was stuck here for the next few hours at least—he'd promised to take her back to the hospital to see her mum, which meant he had a period of being here…alone with Ivy. He could manage a few hours. Just. Then he would get the hell out and back to the sanitised sanity of his chaotic but uncomplicated life.

In the meantime, he had to make the most of this unexpected downtime. Inching his way from underneath the soggy furball, crawling out of bed and shrugging on some running gear, he left the house in silence to explore what wonders York had to offer. A leafy path opposite the front door headed off next to a slow flowing river, towards what looked like the business centre. What better way to put a woman out of your mind than by sprinting through a new city?

The air was fresh and crisp and rich with something sweet—something delicious, like sugar candy. It made his gut curl with hunger. But again, as with thoughts of Ivy, he put everything aside and focused his effort into each footfall. Few people were out and about this early so he was able to up his pace and circumnavigate what appeared to be an old city surrounded by ancient, crumbling walls and lush greenery.

Weak sunshine fought its way through light grey clouds. It was quiet, the cobbled streets were deserted, and his mind began to settle a little with the rhythmic thud of each step.

An hour later, and much calmer, he found her in the lounge curled up on a window seat that overlooked a typical country garden filled with the fragrant blooms of spring flowers. Her laptop was open and files were scattered around her feet. She was wearing dark blue pyjamas and had wrapped a thick cream woollen cardigan around herself, and his heart clutched a little to see her working so early. Seemed the woman had so much to prove. Too much.

Even though she'd been out of his head briefly while he'd pondered some historical ruins likely put there by some old Roman ancestor of his, she settled firmly back into it the moment he set eyes on her again.

She jumped a little as she realised he was watching her, her eyes narrowing, breath quickening. 'Matteo! Gosh, you must have been up early.'

'*Buongiorno*. I had a strange companion with his own quirky alarm.' If he went to her he might just kiss her good morning. So he stayed exactly where he was, at the door.

'Ah. Yes. Hugo. Sorry about him. He's a free-loader and body heat is his catnip. You should have just kicked him off and turned over.'

'The cat wasn't for kicking.'

'No, you're probably right. He's like you. Stubborn and wilful. Now, there's coffee in the press. Just put a light under it. Actually…' She slapped the lid of her laptop down and swivelled to a stand. Her toes were painted a bright pink that matched her cheeks. And why he noticed such a small, innocuous detail he couldn't say. 'I can finish up for

a few minutes if you like. Make you some breakfast. It's the least I can do for you. Where did you
get to on your run?'

Sticking firmly to the wall, he tried to remember a route that he hadn't paid a great deal of attention to. 'I stuck to the river path into town, took
a detour to see some of the old black and white
buildings with the overhanging top storeys and the
sagging middles, had a look at the ruined walls,
and went down past the railway museum. Pretty
place all in all.'

'Well, that at least means I don't have to worry
about showing you round, apart from the Minster
and a proper walk through the Shambles—you've
got to go see them, everyone else does. You can't
come here and not see all the most famous bits.'
She smiled and it was like sunshine, warming and
welcome. He cringed internally at that thought.
He was getting too soft. All that work at harden-
ing his heart and she had to start melting it.

No.

It wasn't going to happen. 'You don't have to
worry about me. You're here for your mum. I've got
calls to make as it is—I need to check up on Joey.'

Busily stacking her files into a pile, she looked

up at him. 'Oh, yes. Let me know how he's doing. And you're going to miss your game. I feel very guilty.'

'Don't waste your energy. Stay where you are, you're working. I can fix myself something.'

'I feel guilty about that too. And about not getting enough work done. I'd planned to get through so much this weekend. I've just phoned the ward to see how Mum's doing and the nurse said she was comfortable and asking for some breakfast.' She walked through to the kitchen, flicked the heat under a stovetop coffeepot. Then turned to him, biting her bottom lip.

'Matteo, how am I going to manage to work while I'm here? I know this sounds really mean and very selfish, but I need to be in London. And I need to be here for my mum. I can't do both. How do people juggle these things?'

His eyebrows rose. 'It's very important, this sexual harassment case?'

'It is to the three women making it. And to the guy who could lose his job and reputation if it turns out he's been falsely accused—although I doubt it. It's a delicate issue and I need to be there.'

'Work, work, work. You have to learn to put

yourself first. Put family first.' God forgive him for that. Because when it came to family he chose not to be there too. 'Is there anyone else who could fill in?'

The coffee fizzed and spluttered and she decanted it into two cups. 'I have a junior, but he's still very inexperienced. Becca's my assistant, but I don't really know her strengths as yet and this is too important to get wrong. I'd wanted to go through it all with her, have her watch how I do things. Besides, work is me. I am work. And that sounds really sad. But at least it's clear cut. There's nothing confusing about getting up every morning and heading in to the office. No room for anything else, like extraneous distractions.'

No room for a life. And that was the way he liked it too, although he was starting to wonder just what he was missing. He trotted out the line he gave his overworked junior staff. 'Life's all about the stuff that's not work, too. No wonder you end up so strung out. Ivy, there is so much more, you just have to give yourself a chance. Couldn't you postpone the case?' When she didn't answer he touched her arm. 'Ivy? Couldn't they put it off? How long do you think you need to be here?'

She shrugged. 'You're the doctor. How long does she need?'

'You're the daughter. Same question.' It was a challenge that seemed to hit home, but she didn't show that she understood his inference. It wasn't his place to tell her what was important in her life. *Mio Dio*, who was he to judge?

Her smile was genuine. 'Did anyone ever tell you that you're a giant insufferable pain in the backside?'

'All the time.'

'Does it make a difference?'

He fluttered his eyelashes at her. 'What do you think?'

'That you make me crazy.' She threw her hands in the air in an exasperated gesture that was more Italian than English. He liked it. She made him laugh. She turned him on. Plain and simple.

None of this was simple, he was realising. 'I think you were crazy long before you met me.'

'You, Matteo, are everything I hate about men. You're bossy and...well, bossy. And, well, let's just say you annoy me. A lot.'

So funny, because she was very definitely not annoyed right now. She was hot and sweet and looking like she needed kissing again. He caught her chin between his thumb and forefinger and pulled her to look at him. 'Aha. But still you kissed me. And not just once.'

'I was trying you out. Sizing you up.' This close to that pouting mouth he was very tempted to do it again.

'And what?'

'And nothing. Absolutely nothing.' She flapped a hand at his chest and it struck ever so lightly against his skin. He caught her wrist and she turned full into him, so close he caught her scent mingling with the smell of her shampoo. Saw the dark green of her eyes, the honeyed flecks, all golden and melting. God, she was breathtaking. He wanted to kiss her. To have her, right now, here on the kitchen table. Wanted to be inside her. He wanted her with a passion he'd never had for anyone, ever.

A little dalliance would be fun, but then what? At what cost to both of them? Neither wanted… *anything* from anyone else. They were two islands of independence with a large ocean of complication between them.

So he tried to make it playful, dropped her hand,

gave her a smile. 'Okay, so take me out for breakfast. And I want to see the Minster that everyone's
so keen on showing me.'

She stepped back and held her wrist—not in
pain, no, he hadn't hurt her—but she just held it
close to her chest. Her voice was sultry and shaky,
as if she'd just had the best sex of her life—or
wanted to. 'Yes. Good idea, let's go outside. First,
phone about Joey?'

Matteo looked down at his running gear. 'No.
First a shower. I need to get out of these things.'

'A shower. Okay. Shower...water...over your
body...' Her gaze scanned his face slowly from his
eyes to his mouth, where it lingered. The memories of those kisses hovered in the silence. Heat
rose within him. Need curled through the kitchen,
thick and heavy and tangible.

He took a step back. 'I'll go now.'

'Yes. Do.'

This thing was getting more intense, like a
flame that had suddenly erupted into life and
was consuming everything in its path, blazing a
trail between them. He needed to get away from
her before he did something stupid. Like kiss her

again. If he didn't douse himself in cold water he wouldn't be able to function around her.

'Wait!' She walked towards him, the cardigan slipping from her shoulders and falling to the floor. Without a word she walked up the stairs and he followed her, hungry to see what she was doing. Was she going to...? Did she want...? A shower? With him? Was this the beginning?

His heart began a strange thumping against his ribcage and for the first time in his life he felt less than sure of his next move.

She stopped short at a door, turned to look at him and gave him a smile, eyebrows cocked. Then she dragged the door open, reached in and pulled out... 'Towels, Matteo. I forgot to give them to you last night.'

Mio Dio. He'd thought he was going to have a heart attack. And now she was so close to him he wanted to touch her. To run his fingers through her hair. To feel that soft skin against his. He was hot and hard for her. Every part of him strained for her.

Holding the towels at hip level, he cursed the flimsy running shorts. 'Thanks. I'll go. Now...'

'Just so you know, the shower's a bit temperamental. Turn the cold water on first then adjust the hot to suit you. That is…' Glancing towards his nether regions, she gave him a wry but cheeky smile that was so not the buttoned-up Ivy he knew—but was a whole lot more of the Ivy he wanted to get to know. 'If you want hot at all.'

The cardiac care ward was locked. Ivy pressed the intercom button and waited. And waited some more. Inside she could see a blur of people running along the corridor. *Running.* To the blare of a siren. *Crap.* Her hand hit her mouth as her heart developed a fast, jerky rhythm. 'What's happening? What is it?'

She knew what it was.

Matteo's hand slipped into hers. 'It's an emergency. Crash call, I imagine. It's okay, Ivy. They're all experts.'

'Do you think…?' *It's my mum?* She couldn't get the words out. Pain crushed her chest as she held her breath.

'Try not to think at all.' With a gentle smile that shone through his eyes he cradled her head against his chest and she inhaled his now familiar scent, which steadied her nerves. He was solid and strong and she felt safe with him. Apart from the fact that there was an emergency in there. And she was out here. That pain intensified. 'Put your arms around me,' he said softly.

'No.' She didn't know whether she'd be able to let go. Whether holding on tight was giving him the wrong message. So, digging deep inside herself, she steadied her reactions. She'd managed this far in her life without needing anyone else. She could manage some more.

He shook his head and took her hand. 'Don't think about it, just do it. Hold on.'

'Oh.' Her defences worn down, her grip on her mum's bag lessened. The bag dropped to the floor. Ivy did as she was told, wriggling her arms round his waist, feeling the breadth of him, his warmth. 'I'm scared.'

'I know.' He didn't give her any pithy pep talks about how fine she would be, how everything would be okay, he just held her. And for that she was grateful. She just took strength from him. Leaning against him, she felt the regular beat of his heart, the unrushed intake of breath. The safety net that she knew would be willing to hold her up if she needed it.

And she wondered what it would be like to be part of something. To be a half of a whole. If that could even happen. All that *you complete me* stuff wasn't real, was it? It was something her mum had been looking for her whole life, and had never found. All those wasted years of chasing a ghost.

No, maybe it wasn't real. But it felt damned nice to be held like this in her worst moments. She'd never had that—not from anyone. Someone to be with her and focus just on her. Someone who seemed to know what she needed without her having to tell them, without her having to strive for their attention.

Eventually the alarm stopped. The rushing slowed and after a few minutes a smiling doctor came to the door. 'Oh, were you waiting? So sorry. Come on in.'

An air of calm pervaded the place. It was as if the running hadn't happened. Or as if the doctor took everything in his stride. Like Matteo. So Ivy tried to stop herself from running too. 'If something bad had happened they'd have stopped me from coming in, right? Surely? They'd take me to one side?'

Matteo nodded. 'Of course. You think too much, like you expect something bad to happen.'

'Well, I just want to be prepared if it does.' Her mum was standing, in an old faded hospital nightie and dressing gown, at the side of her bed, smiling and chatting to a man about her age. Ivy almost ran to her in relief. 'Hey, Mum. Thank God. You look a lot better today, up and about even.'

Her mum's face brightened as she gave a hesitant smile. 'Oh, yes, well, you always look better when they get rid of some of the tubes. This is Richard. He's visiting my neighbour in bed eight. Funnily enough, he lives on West Mews, just round the corner from us.'

From you. Ivy didn't live there any more. It wasn't home. Hadn't ever been, really. And what now? Her mum chatting someone up already— she really was getting back to normal. 'Hi, Richard. Mum, what was going on before? That alarm? All those doctors rushing around? That wasn't… that wasn't for you?'

'Oh, that. It was someone in the first bay. Poor chap. I'll be happy when they move me off here.'

So will I.

'Hello, Mrs Leigh.' Matteo stepped forward and Ivy realised she was still holding his hand and that her mum was looking at her strangely.

Her mum's eyebrows rose. 'Montgomery. Actually, it's Dr Montgomery. But that's okay, you can call me Angela. Everyone does. Has Ivy shown you around the town?'

'Yes. And he was impressed with the Minster, but it's not as beautiful as Siena Duomo, apparently. As if. It's a darned sight older. Or at least the foundations are.' Ivy felt the smile in her voice. She just couldn't help it. Cathedral wars, really? Seemed they had to differ on most things, or rather they both had opinions they liked to air. But it was a good challenge. Kept her on her toes. 'The man's a philistine.'

'I said it was impressive. It is,' he clarified. 'I liked it, truly. It just doesn't have the romance of the Duomo's structure.'

Angela gave him an interested smile, her lips twitching. 'You're right, there. I did love all that marble.' Then she turned back to Ivy. 'Did you bring my things? I need to freshen up.'

'Sure.' Ivy proffered the bag while taking in the

plethora of tubes attached to her mum. 'Do you need any help?'

'Okay. Yes.' Angela's eyes flitted between Ivy and Matteo, and Ivy sensed a mother-daughter talk or something was brewing. Which would be novel. 'Actually, that would be great.'

As her mum hobbled off towards the bathroom, IV stand in tow, Matteo squeezed Ivy's hand and she realised she didn't want to let it go. It was nice to have someone on her side. Which was a whole crock of crazy considering that a couple of weeks ago they'd been at loggerheads. But he gave her a gentle push. 'Off you go. Start now.'

'Start what?'

'Fixing things.'

'What if she doesn't want to?'

He rolled his eyes. 'Would you ever want to look back and regret that you didn't give it a go? Just be honest.'

'She might not want to hear it.'

'How else can you work things through, without honesty?'

'Okay. I s'pose.' He was right. He was often right, goddamn him. Not always…but enough to annoy her just a little bit more. She hid her smile.

As she followed her mum towards the ladies' bathroom she felt his gaze on her back, realising that for the first time in years she hadn't been conscious of her limp—that she was rarely self-conscious when she was with him.

Sensing him still watching her, she injected her gait with a jaunty swing of her bottom. It felt good. Mischievous, and out of character. Or maybe she had a part of her that she'd repressed? Maybe there was a part of her psyche that did want the trappings, the sex, the man? A part that she'd chosen to deny?

Wow. That was an eye-opening thought. But not one she was going to pay any more attention to. She hadn't come this far in her life to give it all up for a life of compromise and dependency.

As if to remind her of that, her mum's bag handle dug into her palm. Ivy tried to ignore those feelings of regret and...well, fear. Fear of feeling things. Of hurting. Of being let down. Of rejection all over again. She'd spent a good deal of her life closing herself off to people. But if Matteo was right, she needed to stop being scared. At least where her mum was concerned.

Let her in.

Let her in.

Let her in.

And she wanted to. She did. She wanted a chance.

'How do I look?' Angela was looking in the mirror and patting her hair, which was matted and flattened at the back. In truth, she looked tired and washed out and old. Blue-red bruises bloomed on her papery skin and her eyes were clouded.

'Like I said, you look great, all things considered, and getting better every day. You've just had a life-saving operation, you're not meant to look like something out of a magazine.' Lifting her mum's arm, threading the IV bag up through her nightgown sleeve and then hanging the fluid bag on the stand, Ivy gave her a smile. 'I was so worried about you.'

'Don't be. I'm fine. Listen, Ivy, I need to talk to you.'

Ivy spoke to her mum's reflection in the mirror. 'Mum, you're healing, you have to take it easy.'

'There's something I need to say.'

'Save it for another time.' Matteo's big honest kick could wait until her mum was feeling better. 'This isn't the time or the place. You're not well.'

'But I need to talk about this.' Angela nodded, still breathless, still pale, but clearly trying to act normal. Whatever that was. 'I know I haven't been easy to live with, Ivy. Things have been hard over the years. Depression has clouded so much, it was so disabling at times. But this scare has made me take stock of things. I want to put things right.'

'Depression?' Ivy had considered that over the years, but her mum had always seemed so content with a man and so unhappy without one that Ivy had thought her mum's moods had been linked entirely with her relationship status at the time. Guilt shook through her again, but sadness too. 'I didn't realise. I should have, but I didn't.'

'You were too busy just being a girl, Ivy. I didn't want to bother you with my problems. But I suspect you lived them anyway?'

Her childhood had been no fairy-tale. She hadn't exactly been shielded from the dramas, especially when her step-family had been ripped away from her. She'd lost her normal, and had been plunged into her mum's darkest moments, borne the brunt of her insecurities.

Even though this conversation was the last

thing Ivy wanted, she nodded. If Angela felt up to saying this—and she really did seem to want to talk—then Ivy needed to let her say it.

Angela looked genuinely sorry. 'I'm sorry. I wasn't very good at all that. I know you got caught in the cross-fire and I leaned on you a lot at times. But I was grateful to have you.'

It never felt like it.

Hurt surged through her. This truth gig wasn't pleasant. In fact, it was downright painful. Ivy didn't want to relive everything that had happened, she just wanted things to be different going forward. Why drag over the old pain? Why not just try to fix things from now? 'I'm sure you did your best.'

'I don't know… Now that I look back, I can see so many mistakes.' Holding onto the sink rim, Angela looked down at her thin hands, then back at Ivy. 'I don't know if we can make things better. Just a little? I don't know…'

'Me neither.' Was it too late for them? Ivy didn't know. What she did know was that she didn't want her mother to die—that had to mean something. Stepping forward, she stroked a hand on Angela's shoulder. 'We could try.' Whatever that meant. There was no blueprint for the next steps they were going to take. Did her mum really mean it? Or would she revert to her old ways once she'd regained some strength?

It was a risk Ivy was willing to take. She pushed away the dark cloud hovering at the back of her mind. Things would be better now. Surely?

Her mum's smile was a little wobbly. 'Yes, I think we should try, Ivy. I'd like to. I'm so glad you're here to stay for a while, we can do some nice mother-daughter things together.'

But, despite wanting to fix everything, Ivy's heart lurched. And, yes, she knew it was terribly self-absorbed to be thinking of herself, but if she stayed too long in York and lost her job then everything she'd worked for would be gone. She'd have no security.

And no seeing Matteo.

That thought bothered her more than she'd thought it would. Over the last couple of days he'd become more than a colleague. Despite his annoying ways. Despite every barrier she'd put up.

But, on the other hand, how could she leave her mum?

Would this time to heal be any different from the rest?

It was the first time they'd ever been so open with each other, that they'd acknowledged out loud that there had been problems. It felt scary. Strange, kind of wobbly, but hopeful. Angela looped her arm into Ivy's as they made their way slowly out of the bathroom, dragging the IV stand with them. 'Your man seems nice.'

'He's not my man.' Ivy lowered her voice— even though he was metres away. Healing the rift with her mother was one thing, but she hadn't envisaged diving straight into confidences about her personal life. 'He's just a friend.'

Angela threw her a sideways look. 'Yes, I hold hands with my male friends too. All the time. And the way you look at him—that's not the way a friend looks at another friend.'

'Oh, no. Really? *Eurgh*. Really?' Was it obvious to everyone? Somewhere along the line he'd wriggled his way under her skin. She cared for him. A fierce panic gripped her chest. 'Great. Brilliant. It's so not the right thing to do.'

Her mum looked at her as if she'd gone mad. 'Calm down. It's not a crime to have a bit of fun.'

'That's just it, Mum. I haven't really done this before and I don't know what to do.' Was she really asking relationship advice from the serial divorcee? Apparently so. 'I don't want anything from him, I don't want a relationship. I just want to do my job and to be left in peace.'

But I do want him. That's the damned problem.

'Hey, don't overthink it like I do—that's the kiss of death to any relationship. Just enjoy it. That's what I'm going to do with Richard, anyway.'

'Richard? Really? You've only just met him.' Ivy came to a halt so the men couldn't hear her. What was her mum saying? She was unbelievable. She hadn't changed a bit, she was the same old lady saying the same old things, doing the same old routine. She'd spent the best part of her working life as a doctor fixing people, but in the end the only person she'd failed to fix was herself.

She's fragile, Ivy reminded herself. She's had a scare and is reaching out for comfort.

Or was she just up to her old tricks again? Her mum needed people around her, she couldn't function on her own, and regardless of anything

Ivy did or said, she couldn't change that. Happiness was fleeting, she'd learnt. And if Richard made Angela happy, even for a short while, who was she to interfere?

But she needed to say how she felt, just to know that she'd tried to protect her mum from yet another relationship disaster. 'You're in hospital. You had a heart scare. A serious medical problem. You can't start flirting with someone's visitor.'

'Ah, there you go again, overthinking. To tell you the truth, Ivy, I'm lonely, I need a little companionship. It's not as if you're living next door, popping round for sugar every other day. You're miles away and I never get to see you.' Angela gave Ivy's hand a pat. 'And that's you through and through, always so independent, doing your own thing, forging your way in the world. You never accepted any help from being about four years old. I have no idea where you got that from.'

Necessity. 'My dream job is in London, Mum, I have to go where the work is. I'm sorry I can't be here all the time, but that doesn't mean you have to jump into a…friendship…with the first person you meet. You need to be careful. Remember what happened with the others...' The tears, the drama.

'Of course I'll be careful, dear. But I need to do what I need to do, too. I just want some company. It's not a lot to ask for after everything I've been through. Really, darling, I know we've never done the heart-to-heart thing, but when you're ready I can listen. Mind you, don't ask my advice. I'm useless with men.'

'Oh?' Ivy threw her a smile. There was only so much she could say or do to stop her mum following her well-trodden path. Angela seemed undeterred. 'I hadn't noticed.'

When they arrived back at the bed Matteo and Richard were discussing something to do with an article in an open newspaper on the table. Matteo looked up as she arrived, helped her settle her mum back in bed, all concern and interest and polite nodding.

He'd been so nice Ivy wanted to give something back, even if it meant sacrificing something for herself. Drawing him to one side, she whispered, 'Matteo, I know you're probably thinking about heading off back to London soon, but I wondered—when we've done here, could we go to the pub? Watch the game on TV? What do you think?'

Those dark stubborn eyes glinted. 'I was going to listen to it on the sports radio on the drive back.'

'Oh. Well, that's okay, then.' Disappointment rattled through her. She had an insane desire to spend just a few more minutes with him. 'I feel as if the last two days have been all about me. You've sacrificed your days off to be here, I just thought it would be a way of saying thank you. It's not... I don't want you to get the wrong impression. It's just a pub, maybe some food. The game. I'm not offering any more than that.'

Was it her imagination, or did he look just a little relieved? 'Well, I would prefer to watch it than listen to it. But what about your work? I thought you had too much to do already?'

She shrugged. 'So maybe I can take a little time off? Just a couple of hours.'

His eyebrows rose in surprise. 'Whoa. Watch out, Ivy Leigh, you might get into the habit of relaxing. Then what would happen?'

Staring into his eyes, his heated gaze focused

on her, she felt relaxed and excited and scared and comfortable all at the same time. This man was too easy to fall for and she was tumbling deeper and deeper. But she could handle it. She'd laid out the parameters. 'I can't imagine, Matteo. I just can't imagine.'

CHAPTER NINE

'COME ON, ENGLAND! Yes! Yes! Yes! Go!'

So this was the unleashed version of Ivy Leigh? Matteo laughed as she stood, eyes glued to the huge wall-hung TV in the sports pub, body tensed and fists punching the air. 'God,' he groaned into his pint. 'This is terrible. Less than an hour ago you did not know a thing about rugby. Now look at you—England's most fervent fan.'

High-fiving the two open-mouthed English supporters at the next table, she beamed. 'This is fun. We're beating you, Matteo, that's all that matters.'

'There's time yet.' He shrugged, far more entertained by her reactions than the game.

'You think? In the history of the Six Nations championship there have been over twenty games between England and Italy, and England have won them all. Your chances are zero, Mr Hero.'

'Twenty games—how the hell…? Since when did you know that?'

'The wonders of the internet. You just have to know where to look.' She winked at him. 'I did my research. You didn't think I'd invite you to watch a game we had the remotest chance of losing, did you?' On-field action caught her attention again, she paused, breathing heavily as her eyes glued themselves to the game. 'Come on, mate. Pass it. Yes. Yes!'

Thank God for half-time. She sat down, all flushed and hot-cheeked, her chest heaving with excitement. 'This is brilliant. Why did no one ever tell me that watching sport was such fun?'

He drained his glass and put it back on the table. The fun was in watching her watching the game. 'It is when you're winning. And I have to say you are very entertaining.'

She patted his arm condescendingly. 'Poor pet, you're a very sore loser. But still glad you came?'

'To watch you beat us? No.' *Yes.* But he was confused as all hell now. He should have gone when he'd had a chance, instead of being drawn in by those large green eyes sparkling so coyly at him, offering *no more* than a game of rugby. And despite every brain cell screaming at him to climb into the car and head down the motorway, he'd grabbed the chance for a couple more hours with her, like a starving man thrown paltry crumbs.

Her tongue darted out to moisten her lips and he was mesmerised by the action, every part of him wanting to taste her. She gave him a smile. 'I mean, are you glad you came to York? I know it wasn't exactly for your benefit but I hope it hasn't been too bad.'

'What? Spending my non-hospital hours in a hospital, not sleeping with a ginger cat that purrs like a drill? Sure, it has been the best weekend ever.' He felt a laugh rumbling from his throat. Being here with her, on the other hand… 'And now we are losing. It is getting better all the time.'

'I hope it does, for your sake. Although I'm not sure I want to give up that win—so you'll have to find something else to make you smile.'

He let that thought hover for a while, not wanting to admit the way he was feeling so conflicted about how much she made him smile. 'It's too late, Ivy. The weekend is doomed.'

'Oh, poor sweetheart. Things can only get better. So, tell me, when did you come to live in England, and why?'

He did a quick mental calculation. 'It was about

six years ago. I wanted to work with Dave Marshall, he has such a great international reputation—the very best and cutting-edge work in our field—so when we met at a conference in Milan and he invited me to join his team, I jumped at the chance. I haven't looked back.'

'And you already spoke English? I'm impressed.'

'I was pretty rusty. We had learnt it at school from a young age, but even so I was pretty terrible when I first got here. It has been a steep learning curve.'

'I'll bet. Where did you train to be a doctor?'

So she wanted his life history, which was fine by him. He could give her a short version and veer away from anything that might make her ask deeper questions. 'In Florence. Then I went to Milan to specialise, they have a great renal unit there.'

She took another drink of wine. 'You said you don't go home. Why not?'

Straight to the point. Now he wished he hadn't encouraged her to be like this. 'I see you have taken notice of your lawyer training, you have... how do you say it? Cut to the chase. You can do it to me but not for yourself.'

'That, my boy, is called self-preservation.' She twiddled with the stem of the glass then focused her gaze at him again, which made him hot under the collar. 'Now answer my question. Why don't you go home?'

'I'm too busy. Work takes up my time. And there's not a lot there for me.'

'What, a whole load of siblings and parents? That's a lot of reasons to go home.'

Not enough. 'Some of them come here. I see them. Liliana, my little sister with the renal problems, lived with me for a year in London. You can imagine how much fun that was. She is years younger and about five times the trouble of all the others put together.'

'But you love her, I can tell.' Ivy smiled again. It was sweet and soft and real and for a moment he wanted to do nothing but stare at that mouth.

'Of course I love her.' And now he had time to think about it, he did miss the closeness they'd all had, growing up. But betrayal had blown a hole into that that could never be healed. He'd purposely left them all to their lives and chosen disconnectedness. That way he would remain intact, heart and soul. To go home would be to have a constant reminder of what had happened.

But, of course, Ivy did not need to know any of this. Why go deep when this was not that sort of relationship?

This was a weekend for her to be with her family, not for him to get intense about his. Or intense about anything, for that matter, or to lose himself at the whim of emotions that he knew never lasted.

Ivy ran a hand across her blonde hair and fluffed it up nonchalantly. She didn't seem to care that it stuck up in tufts. She had stopped hiding her limp. She was cheering like a madwoman. He was seeing a very different Ivy from the one at work. She was letting her guard down; was that a good sign, or a dangerous one? He had a bad feeling it was the latter. And all he knew was that she was in his head and he couldn't get her out of it.

'Don't you miss it all, though, Matteo? Your family. The sunshine. Decent food. Blue sky. All that wine. Amazing architecture. Art…? Nah, there's nothing there at all for you, is there? God, I'd love to live in Italy.'

'You have a very touristy image of my home.'

Which was indeed all the things she'd mentioned but with a large dose of reality. And feuding families. And hurt. 'But now you come to mention it, I guess it does have a few things going for it. Decent coffee, for a start. Although you do have some pretty amazing architecture here too. The Minster is stunning, with its stained glass, and the intricate carving and the history.'

'Yeah, right. Just not marble enough?' After she'd signalled to a glass collector and given a repeat order for beer and wine she turned back to him. 'What do your parents do?'

He shrugged. 'So clichéd. A small taverna. My mum's the…I suppose you'd call it the maitre d'. She makes it work, ruling with a fist of iron. My dad is the chef. We all did our time there, growing up, in the kitchen, waiting tables.'

She eyed him suspiciously, eyes narrowing. 'What's the problem with your dad?'

'What do you mean?' But he was aware that he had become tense and tried to loosen his shoulders.

'Your voice changed, you paused. Your eyes narrowed. Your shoulders are trying to break for freedom. You're not the only one who can ace elementary psychology. You have father issues.'

No, he'd solved them years ago and never looked back. 'He's not worth wasting your time over. None of it is. Live in the now, Ivy. Oh, look, the game's beginning again.'

Her eyes flicked to the TV screen and back to him again. 'Sod the game.'

Forcing a smile he shook his head. 'Ivy, Ivy, you are too…what is the word?…fickle. I thought you were the world's biggest rugby convert?'

'Not when there are more interesting things to talk about.'

Thankfully the waiter brought their drinks, buying Matteo some time. He took a long drink and tried to watch the game. But he'd underestimated her. She nudged him. 'Your dad?'

'Trust me, my past is not interesting.'

'It is to me.'

That was an admission. Her eyes clashed with his and he saw the moment she also realised the enormity of what she had just said.

What the hell was happening here he didn't know. Because he was as shocked as she was. Right when part of him was keeping that door slammed closed there was a part of him that wanted to talk. That wanted out-and-out openness. It wasn't that he had made a solemn vow never to talk about it, he just hadn't ever wanted to expose so much of his damaged past.

This was neither the right time nor the right place. 'You need to focus on yourself. On healing things with your mum, on how you're going to do your job next week. And the fact we just scored a try while you weren't paying attention. Now we are drawing. England are on the run.'

She looked at him for a long time. Long enough for Italy to miss the conversion. For them to stay just behind their opponents.

Nothing was said. She didn't push. She didn't nag him, she let him off. Which was the sweetest thing she could do right then, when he didn't want his past interfering with this moment. It seemed she knew when to ask, when to stop. She knew every damned button he had and pressed them all. Too much.

Something shifted in his chest, something momentous. Something real. Something he hadn't been looking for and didn't know if he wanted. In fact, something that scared the hell out of him because he'd felt similar things before and it had ended horribly. He didn't want anything close to that happening again. He needed to get away from here. From her.

He sat back in his seat, putting distance between himself and the woman who he knew was taking up more of his heart and his head than she should. But Ivy didn't seem to notice, fixed her eyes on the game.

She wasn't quiet for long.

'Come on, boys. Come on. That's it. Pass it out. To the left. Yes! *Yes!* We won! You beauty!' She jumped up, turned, squeezed his cheeks between her thumb and forefinger and kissed him on the lips, hard and fast. And another. 'Beat that, Matteo.'

For a second he stilled. He didn't want to touch her.

Could not. Would not.

Who was he kidding? No matter what he thought, his body was hell-bent on betraying him at every turn. He wanted her.

It was a normal, natural attraction. It didn't have to mean more than that. It didn't have to be dangerous. He was worrying over nothing. He'd had sex many times with many women and he'd made sure he'd got out with his heart unscathed. He could do that with Ivy, couldn't he?

He was through thinking about it, he was getting as bad as she was.

'Oh, no, you don't get away that easily.' Yanking her towards him amongst the cheering supporters who had all left their seats, he gripped her waist. Planted another kiss on her lips. Then another. My God, she tasted divine. Heat shimmied through him, heat and need. Hot and hungry.

She wrapped her arms around his neck and deepened the kiss with equal hunger. Her body pressed against his, curling into him. When she wriggled her hips against his erection he felt her sigh. With a dirty smile she pulled away but kept a grip on his arm, her words forced out. 'Sod the game. Sod everything. Matteo, do you have to go home tonight?'

'Typical northern weather.' For an early evening the sky was dark. Heavy clouds loomed overhead, threatening a downpour. Ivy's hands were shaking as she stepped out into the thick raindrops that began to fall. This was so out of her comfort zone. She didn't do this. She didn't straight up ask a man to come back to her place. She didn't have wanton sex. She never made a move, first or otherwise. Her heart jittered as she quickened her pace, more out of a desire not to lose her nerve than anything else. 'Come on, we'll have to hurry or we'll get soaked.'

Matteo was uncharacteristically quiet as they headed down the river path to her mum's house. Slipping his hand into hers, he pulled her against him. Rain fell in relentless waves feeding the swollen river, water dripping in gullies between their layers of clothes.

'Ivy.' His eyes were dark and intense and misted. And she knew from one look that he wanted her, wanted this as much as she did. There was a promise between them, silent and yet overt. Dangerous. Dark. So very sexy. One step over an invisible line. Her tummy danced and curled and tightened as the sexy look in his eyes seemed to reach into her gut and tease.

He ran his thumb down her cheek, traced a path over her bottom lip.

She bit down.

His eyes grew darker, hotter. His body tensed. *'Mi fai impazzire.'*

She groaned. 'What are you saying? Please, tell me that means come to bed.'

'Almost. It means you make me crazy.'

'It could mean *two tickets to Leeds, please,* and I swear I wouldn't care, I just love how you sound. Say more…'

'Sei cosa bella. Due biglietti per Leeds, per favore.'

'Yes. Yes. Anything you want.' Without thinking further than this moment, she pulled him towards her, fixed her mouth on his and tasted him again. Maybe it was the wine that had relaxed her reserve but she felt tipsy with desire, filled with a need that seemed to become more intense, more breathtaking every time she looked at him.

As she heard a moan coming from her throat she was shocked by the spiralling need at her core. She wanted this man. So much. Too much. Her hands circled his waist, palm flattening against that famous backside. With a sudden rush of excitement she pressed herself against him. She wanted to feel every inch of him against her. Naked. Wet.

She began to explore the taut ridges of his back,

hands running over wet linen that stuck to a body she'd dreamt about, that she'd seen butt naked on a screen. Until now out of reach, but still stalking her thoughts. Now it was real. It was real and she wasn't going to think too deeply about it. She was going to do what her mother said…she was going to enjoy it. She was going to not overthink it.

Her mother…good God. Ivy felt her body shut down.

No way in hell.

Her heart pounding fast and hard, Ivy turned away from him, away from the path, and strode towards the road. It was slippery and cold and she tried to concentrate on putting her weight onto her right foot but her head was filled with Matteo and his kisses and the wrongness and the rightness. And she was so torn and muddled. The only thing she knew with any clarity was that she wanted to kiss him. To hold him. And that, for so many reasons, seemed the worst course of action.

'Ivy?' His voice was behind her.

'I'm sorry, Matteo. I just need to go home.' She knew she was being a jerk. But she couldn't do this. Not with him. Not if it meant she was following in her mother's footsteps. She had to take some time out to think about what the hell she was doing at all. If she was going to do anything, she'd do it on her own terms.

'Wait. Ivy. Stop! Sto—!'

She kept her head down and eyes fixed forward. 'Ivy!'

It was fear, not anger she could hear in his voice. Fear? What the—? 'What's wrong?'

As she turned she felt a thump against her body, and at the same time she heard a screech and a scream. Then pain seared through her leg. Someone flew across her path. A whirr of wheels filled the air and a crash. A bicycle? A man on a bicycle?

Off now. On the ground. Shouting at her. Her leg hurt.

Blood was starting to drip from his knee. His face was scrunched up. There was blood. Uh-oh. What did she have to do? Breathe? Tense? Relax? She couldn't remember.

Breathe.

Matteo? Where was Matteo?

Strong, warm arms circled her, lifting her off the road as her knees buckled and her vision began to swim.

'Ivy. What the hell? Are you crazy?' Matteo was

sitting her down on the kerbside, his hands on her leg, on her foot, ripping her shoe off. She didn't have the energy to stop him. 'Are you okay? Ivy?'

She swallowed the pain and didn't look at the man with the bike. It was her fault.

All her fault. She'd spent her whole life being cautious and this one time…this was her fault. She should have been more careful. Right from the get-go. Right from the second she'd downloaded that picture. She should have been more careful.

She did a mental body scan. Her leg hurt, more than usual, but she wasn't badly injured. 'Yes. Yes, I'm fine. You'd better go and see the man. I didn't see him. He came out of nowhere. He wasn't there and then he was.'

'He didn't have any lights on. In this weather.' Matteo glanced towards the guy on the ground. The whirring of the wheels were slower now. The man groaned. 'Please. Help me.'

Within an instant Matteo was gone from her side, giving her time to take stock. Every time she let herself go just a little, something happened to remind her of the folly of her actions.

'Ivy.' Matteo's voice was the one he used in the operating theatre. 'Ivy. I need you to focus.'

'Y-yes?'

'Call an ambulance. *Now*. Then come here and give me help.'

'Okay.' As rain teemed down and soaked through to her skin she did as she was asked, telling the ambulance receiver their location. Her hands wouldn't stop shaking and her body felt as if it had gone into shock. She tried to take a few breaths to steady herself, her voice, mirroring Matteo's demeanour when in medical scenarios. She would not think about the blood dripping from the man's head. 'What is the injury?' she called over to Matteo. 'Head injury? Broken arm?'

His voice was too casual as he undid his trouser belt and fashioned a sling around the man's wrist and neck. 'Tell them it looks like a...' He slowed down his speaking so she could understand and repeat his words. 'A displaced clavicle fracture. A bump to his head, a laceration. No loss of consciousness. Tell them it would be really great if they got here pretty soon.' Then he turned to the man. 'Okay, mate. Sit up and take a few deep breaths. The ambulance will be here soon. You'll be fine.'

'It hurts like hell,' the man groaned, as he sat on

the opposite kerb to Ivy, Matteo's hands guiding him into place but supporting the elbow and taking it very slowly so as not to jolt his collarbone.

Ivy limped across the road, her left foot bruised and becoming more sore as she put weight on it. The man's collarbone looked misshapen at its mid-point. But it wasn't sticking out, as she'd assumed it might. It looked as if it had buckled in on itself. 'I'm so sorry.'

'Yeah. You should…watch where…you're going.' Their patient heaved out between breaths. 'But I should have…had lights on…I know. I know…'

'Save your energy, both of you.' Matteo interceded. 'What is done is done. We now have to get this fixed. And quickly.'

Something about his tone had Ivy looking over at Matteo. His eyes were darkened and his jaw taut. There was something more here that she didn't understand. But he clearly couldn't discuss it in front of…

'What's your name?' she asked, trying to keep the conversation light, and to keep the man focused on something other than his injury. He grimaced, his eyes fluttering closed as he spoke. 'Pete. Pete O'Donnell.'

'Well, Pete.' She smiled at him, digging as deep as she could into her failing reserves. 'I don't suppose you caught the rugby game today?'

He shook his head. 'No. I was…going home… to watch…it. Win? Or lose?'

'A great seventeen-fifteen win.'

Matteo gave a hollow laugh. 'Depends who you support.'

'He's Italian,' she explained, hoping to keep Pete interested enough to forget a little of his pain and shock. 'And not particularly happy. But, really, they played well. It was touch and go at one point.'

In the distance a siren blared shrill and welcome. It came closer and closer and louder and louder and Ivy could see Pete starting to become agitated. Mixed with her relief was a little bit of panic. 'If you can just hang on a bit longer, they'll have something to help with the pain.'

Pete tried to push her away with his elbow. 'I think I'm going to be sick.'

'Okay.' She rubbed her palm gently up and down his back. 'It's shock setting in. Take some deep breaths. In. That's it…' She watched as he followed her lead. 'Great. Now out. In again…'

Within seconds the paramedics were out of the

ambulance and giving him some gas and air to help with the pain. Within minutes they'd stabilised his injury, stemmed the bleeding from his grazed head and loaded him into the ambulance. Within half an hour she was alone again with Matteo, facing the real reason this whole sorry scenario had played out. She'd wanted to kiss him so badly it had frightened her.

Her heart hammered. 'God, that was awful.' Now her hands began to shake again as the images of broken bones and blood flitted back into her brain. 'I wish I'd seen him.'

'It is dark and raining and he had no lights. How can he expect to ride on a cobbled street in those conditions and not get hurt? But…' Matteo took her arm and prised her gently from her seated position to standing. 'He's gone and is going to be fine. But you? Not so much? Tell me what the hell was going on.'

'I was in a hurry to get back.'

'Yes? But because you wanted to get away from me.' His hands clenched and he shook his head. 'One minute you were willing, the next you were running away. I don't understand.'

'Mixed messages. I'm so sorry. That wasn't my intention. I just got a little spooked.'

He shook his head. 'You should have told me what you were feeling. Talked to me, Ivy. Not run out into the road. Especially with your leg being so damaged. It could have been serious for you too.'

'I did not run. I was walking. And I looked before I crossed.' She took his arm and tried not to wince as they turned the corner towards her mum's place. 'I don't care about my leg and neither should you.'

'I don't care about your leg. No, I do care. I mean I don't care about how it looks. But now it hurts and I don't want to see you in pain because of me.' He stopped and took her by the shoulders to face him. 'What is the matter?'

How honest could she be with him without making herself vulnerable? 'I don't know. I panicked, suddenly. I didn't know what I was doing.'

'You were kissing me. And it was good. And now you're shivering and we're both soaked and a man has a potentially life-threatening injury.' His thumb ran across her cheek, and his eyes were concerned as he gazed at her. He wasn't cross, as she'd thought he might be.

Even so, her stomach felt as if it had dropped to her toes. 'Was it really bad? I thought you were worried, I could tell by your voice. But you stayed so calm.'

'And you managed to distract him while I stemmed the bleeding and stabilised the break. We were a great team. And you didn't flinch at the blood—too much. A major step forward.' His eyebrows rose and did she see just a little pride there simmering in his pupils? 'His collarbone broke inwards—it could have punctured a blood vessel or his sternum. He may have—we don't know. But it was an emergency in any case.'

'Thank God you were there. I feel so bad.' She bit her lip as she thought. How honest should she be? It felt as if the inside of her head was about to explode. How she wanted to be free and open and honest with him, to relax into something good. To tell him all her thoughts and feelings, to lay herself bare metaphorically. Because that was when true and mutual trust happened, she imagined. But she was conflicted, fighting, knowing that by opening her heart she would be gifting him a part of herself—and she didn't know if she could do that. If she dared. Because what else would she be tempted to give him? What else would he take from her? But he did deserve some kind of coherent explanation. 'I was thinking about my mum.'

Confusion flared, mixed with a little humour. 'That is not a good sign. You were thinking about other things when you were kissing me. Is my kissing that bad?'

'No, your kissing is wonderful. But I was thinking about how she does things and how I don't want to end up like her. She's so dependent. So needy. I don't want to be like that.' *I don't want to lose myself.*

He peeled his jacket off and hooked it over her shoulders, rubbing his hands up and down her arms. 'And you aren't. You could never be like her. You shouldn't have been thinking about anything except the kiss. You want to try again?'

Yes! At just seeing the look in his eyes, feeling his heat, despite the cold and the rain, she knew without a shadow of a doubt that most of her wanted to do it again. This was so unfair. She was holding onto a very fragile line of sensibility here. Torn between her heart and her head. Between doing the right thing and doing the very wrong one. Although she knew which one would be the most fun. 'I don't know.'

'You need convincing? You are a woman and I am a man and there are things we could do that will make us feel amazing.' Scudding his fingers through his chestnut-coloured hair, he shook his head. '*Mio Dio*, this is the hardest I have ever had to work to get a woman to kiss me. Ever.'

A surge of pride swelled in her chest now. 'Good.'

'Good? How can it be good if we are losing valuable time? We could have been kissing for the last hour. Instead, you want to dissect everything into tiny pieces. It is like you're at a trial and everything's under examination. You want to pick. Pick. Pick.' His fingers tickled her ribs with every pointed word.

Squirming away from him, she giggled. This was supposed to be serious, and he was making her laugh? 'I don't want to pick. I'm just being careful. I'm—' *I'm a coward.*

'Stop talking. You and your words drive me insane. Sometimes you just have to go with your gut feeling. Yes?' The pale light of a streetlamp illuminated him. He was glorious. Tall. Strong. Dark. His head tipped back with a smile that would light up a million rugby stadiums. Just being under his heated gaze made every part of her light up too. Anticipation of his kiss, of his touch, skittered across her skin, then penetrated her body, heating her inside.

She thought about what he was saying. What he was asking of her. Her gut feeling was that he would be a very good lover. That he would look amazing with no clothes on. That she wanted to kiss him, to lose herself in the pleasure he was promising. He was asking, sure, but she had to answer. Everything from this moment rested with her next decision. If she said no then she would live to regret it. The same could be said if she said yes. But she could allow herself one small regret in her life, couldn't she? She remembered a phrase she'd heard once before… Always regret something you've done, not something you haven't. She made herself say the word. 'Yes.'

'*Buono.*' Sliding his arm underneath her knees, he stooped and picked her up. 'Now stop the talking. Let's get some action happening.'

'Hey, what the hell do you think you're doing?' Although she didn't try to too hard to stop him.

He shrugged as he walked up the path to her house, carrying her as if she was no weight at all. 'You are cold and wet and shivering. You have an injured foot...'

'It's not that bad...'

'Humour me. Perhaps if I take the lead and make you want me so bad you won't think so much?'

'So bad? No, Matteo, the word is bad*ly*.'

With that he stopped short and grimaced. 'Yes, it's official, you will drive me completely insane.'

Then he plastered her mouth with his, whipping her breath away, along with any further thought process. His kiss was greedy. Hard. Long. Everything she imagined a perfect kiss would be. When he pulled away he was grinning, and breathing heavily. 'But I'm quite happy to go mad if it means I can make you moan again.'

CHAPTER TEN

'ER…MATTEO…' SHE was laughing so hard now she could hardly draw breath. 'That's not the bedroom.'

Opening the bathroom door with a single push of his hips, he tipped her onto the tiles, where she landed feet first. He steadied her. 'A shower first? I'm freezing, and it's one way to heat up. And I thought maybe we just need to start again—with a clean slate.'

'Ooh. Are your jokes as bad in Italian as they are in English?' Her heart was pounding, every nerve-ending was on fire. She didn't need heating up—she was already very, very hot.

Flicking on the tap in the walk-in shower area, he grinned. 'Very bad indeed. Come here.' He pulled her closer, one hand covering hers, the other palming the back of her head as he kissed her again. She gasped as heat and need curled inside her. As he dragged the coat and then her soggy cardigan from her arms his eyes never left her face. 'Yesterday I was in here, praying you would join me. Yesterday I thought you might but I was disappointed. Today I am so glad you are here.'

'Me too. If it's any consolation, I almost did come in here. I was trying to do the right thing. It almost killed me,' she admitted. Her hands fisted his T-shirt, running over dips and curves of muscle, across his chest, down his biceps. She stepped into the shower and pulled him in with her, feeling the most liberated she'd ever felt. Warm water sluiced over them, running in rivulets over their shoulders. And she laughed. It sounded brave, new, echoing across the tiles. Wow. She blinked. So that was what freedom sounded like.

Dragging his T-shirt over his head, she sighed at the sight of his naked torso. My God, he was gorgeous—a heady combination of rippled muscle and tanned skin. She followed the contracting muscles down his chest to his belly. Then her fingers made contact with his jeans waistband. His excitement was evident, and it stoked hers. He wanted her and, *God*, she wanted him. She played a little, running feather finger strokes over his zipper. 'Ah, shucks, now everything's wet. You're just going to have to take these off.'

'Of course. But only if you take these off.' Before she could argue about who should go first, he undid the button on her trousers palmed the fabric and pulled them down. When he reached her feet she lifted one foot then the other and he threw the trousers to one side. On his way back up he stopped briefly to kiss her belly button, the underside of her ribs, her throat. 'My God, Ivy. *Sei cosi bella.*'

So beautiful. And she felt it. For the first time in her life she felt like a goddess. But she was distracted by what she could see. He was every bit as amazing as the picture she'd seen that first morning when her life had been about to fundamentally change. When she'd had no idea what was going to happen; never in her wildest dreams had she thought she would be in such achingly close proximity to that body. Lathering some body wash between her hands, she worked up a decent amount of citrus-scented bubbles.

Running them over his chest in slow circles, her hands kneaded down his abdomen. There were dips there too, a groove she hadn't noticed until now. 'What's this?'

He took her hand and kissed it. 'Nothing. Just an operation scar.'

'Funny place to have an operation.' Looking closer, she found another groove. Across his belly but further down, another. 'They look like bullet holes.'

His laugh reverberated around the room. 'Didn't I teach you anything in my OR? They're laparascope scars. You see? Nothing important.' He took her hand on a journey to each dip then kissed the tips of her fingers. 'You aren't the only one who has lived an interesting life.'

'Mine wasn't interesting. It was just...unusual.' His scars looked pretty. Did he hate them like she hated hers? Did hers look this pretty to him? She doubted that very much. 'From what? What operation?'

'Kiss me again and I'll tell you.' His fingers played over her breasts and for a moment she almost forgot the question. Heat pulsated through her. She wanted to kiss him again. To feel his mouth on hers, to taste him. But she wanted to play too.

'Tell me or I won't kiss you again.'

'Madness. You and your words.' He didn't give her a chance to argue but pushed her against the glass wall and crushed his mouth on hers until she couldn't think straight, until all she wanted to do was touch him. This thing that had been building between them for the last few weeks was so acute, so overpowering. 'I want you, Ivy. I want you too much. You drive me crazy.'

She wasn't going to argue about that. Talking was wasting time. She ran her hands round his waist, grabbed a handful of his bum, making a mental note to ask him later about his scars. Right now she wanted more, she wanted everything he had to offer. With a sharp slap she whacked him on the backside. 'This is the cause of all the trouble. I want to see it. I want to see it right now. I want to see you naked.'

He laughed. 'You already have. The whole world has.'

'Don't I know it.' She pressed herself against him, the water still sluicing over them, the last of the bubbles draining down the plug. 'I want a private audience with your bottom, Mr Finelli. Make it happen.'

'Ah, okay. If you insist.' He turned and began to hum a sexy striptease song as he started to peel his jeans down, a wiggle of the hips, a coy wink, the teasingly slow lowering of his zip. Her mouth watered—every part of her hot. The best private show of her life. *The only one.*

He was the only one.

For a second she hesitated, her heart pounding loud and hard. What did that mean?

She pushed that thought away—no more dissecting things.

Then, her attention firmly back on Matteo's now naked back and...ass...assets, she swallowed. Hard. Her body was simmering. Her core hot. There it was, in all its glory. Peachy indeed. And ripe. God, yes. Extraordinary.

With a quick wiggle he looked over his shoulder, faking the pose from the picture, arms raised against the shower wall. 'Impressive, yes?'

'Hmm, I've seen better.' Oh, holy cow. *If Becca could see me now.* 'Maybe I need a closer look.'

'Feel, I think. Examination is always important. But first...' He turned, fully naked. And she gasped again. He was beautiful. Big. Hard. So damned confident. So dazzling.

Then he, in turn, reached for the shampoo. With slow sensual strokes and in a silence split only by sighs and moans he began to wash her hair, sensually releasing all fear of being here with him, doing this, all shock of the bicycle incident washed away. The shaking that remained came purely from her desire. The quickened breaths only from his touch, from the anticipation of more.

She tried to reach for him through the steam but he shook his head, concentrating on rinsing the shampoo away. Then he started to massage her shoulders, her neck, tantalisingly close to her breasts…nuzzled against her throat, kissing a trail to her collarbone, down to her bra. Which he undid with supreme ease. The man was clearly used to seducing women.

His fingers went lower, caressing her abdomen, her bottom…and he removed her panties… Every part of her strained for his touch. Heat spiralled through her.

Every part of her thrummed with desire. She felt dizzy. To steady herself she grabbed onto his shoulders, reaching, on tiptoe, to give him another kiss. But he had other ideas for his mouth.

When his lips closed around her nipple she thought she had died and gone to heaven. When his fingers slid between her thighs she knew she was definitely there. *Floating.* 'Oh, Matteo. That is...amazing.' She wrapped a leg round his as his stroking became more intense. She wanted him inside her. Wanted him now. Desperation and urgency began to claw through her gut. She was losing...losing all control to his expert touch.

Losing herself...

She could feel his erection against her thigh. Hard and hot. Her fingers closed around it. Now it was his turn to gasp. *'Mio Dio.'*

'Matteo. I need you.' He was so tantalisingly close. 'I need you inside me.'

His forehead rested against hers as his fingers slowed. 'Not yet. Not yet.'

'Now, Matteo. Please. I want you.' She found his mouth again, kissed him hard in a flurry of wet hunger. She bucked against his hand, faster.

'Oh, God.' His eyes shifted from the shower to the door, and back to her. 'Condom...we need...'

Noooooooooo. Don't stop. 'I don't have any.' For a moment she almost didn't care.

The water came to an abrupt stop. He was already out of the shower area. 'In my bag. In the bedroom.'

Shoving past him, she grabbed his hand. 'What are we waiting for?'

'We are all wet.'

'I don't care, Matteo. I just need you.'

That was a thought.

She pushed that away too.

The journey to the bedroom was too long. The faffing with the condom was really too long. But then he was lowering her onto the bed that already smelt of him, and she wanted to sink deep into it and never re-emerge.

'Yeeeogh!'

'What the hell…?' She followed Matteo's jump from the bed as a ginger furball streaked across the room, yowling.

'Your damned cat. My damned butt.' He was peering over his shoulder and rubbing a cheek.

'Oh. No! Not picture perfect any more? It's his bed, I'm afraid. You're just trespassing as far as he's concerned.' Looking at the claw marks indenting those perfect cheeks, she bit back a smile. 'Oh. Goodness. But thank God it was the backside and not the front. Come here and let me kiss it better.'

Eyeing an unrepentant Hugo sitting smugly in the corner, washing one leg with no care in the world, Matteo hissed. 'I do not like making love with an audience.'

Making love. It was too soon, too immense a thing to imagine that that was some place they'd reached. 'I think he wants to show you who is the alpha male.'

'No contest. Hands down. I win. Every time.'

Yes, he did. No argument there. She opened the door and shooed the cat out, then came back to Matteo, spiralling fingers through his hair. 'But I think you have to prove it. I might need some convincing, because up until now Hugo's been the only significant male in my life. Show me how alpha you are.'

'Pah. I have nothing to prove. I'm not fluffy. I'm not fat. And I would never, ever hurt you.' Matteo pulled her to him and smothered her mouth with his and she let herself believe him. Let his fingers work magic, let the doubt fairies creep back into the dark place they'd come from. This time the kiss was slow and deeply sensual. His eyes fixed on hers, so dark and misted and full of something…something deep and honest and true. She couldn't look away. Needed to watch him, to see in his eyes what she knew was mirrored in hers. This was pure. Real. Profound.

The stroke of his tongue against hers sent shock-waves through her, stoking the heat again. Bringing her to fever pitch. 'Matteo.' She didn't know what to say, couldn't find enough words to describe the emotions rippling through her. Enough that everything she thought, everything she felt came down to one word. 'Matteo.'

'Ivy. Ivy…' He wanted her. He called her name. He was losing control. This amazing, accomplished, sexy man was here. With her. For her.

He laid her down on to the bed. Then he was sliding inside her in one deep thrust. And she felt the initial stretch and an intense sharp sting that melted into need. But she still kept watching him, watching that beautiful face showing every nuance of emotion. The intensity of pleasure. The pain of ecstasy. The wonder of such honesty. And she felt every bit as he did. She was raw. Open.

As he increased the pace she went with him. As he began to shake she went with him. Then as he moaned her name over and over again into her mouth she was crashing and flying and soaring with him. And her heart felt as if it had cracked wide open, shifting, making space, letting him in. That last piece of her that wanted to hold back shook loose—tumbling over and over and away until it was barely there, out of reach, so far away, then nothing at all. For a moment panic gripped her. And so she forced herself to look deeper into his eyes, because there, surely, she'd find an answer.

Then she couldn't think at all. She just went with him, giving herself up to this feeling. Losing herself in him.

It was a few minutes before Matteo really had himself under control.

Pah! He wasn't in any kind of control at all. Never had he had such an intense experience. Never had he been so wholly under the spell of a woman. He didn't know what to make of it all, what this feeling in his heart was. It was like a long slow fall into something exciting yet comfortable. To familiarity, and yet a whole new experience of learning. It was exquisite and unique. It was beautiful.

And it scared the hell out of him.

He gave her a soft gentle kiss, his heart lighter when she responded. Cupping her cheek to look at her, he finally managed some words. 'Okay, good, you're still breathing.'

'Only just.'

'That was intense.'

She hesitated before she spoke again. Gathering her breath and, he imagined, her thoughts. What was going through her head? He wondered whether it was messed-up crazy thoughts like his. The pull of intimacy and the push of fear.

Wriggling out from underneath him, she snuggled into the crook of his arm, her head on his chest, blonde hair tickling his nose. 'Yes. That was…just amazing, Matteo. Just amazing.'

'Yes. It was…amazing.' His heart was too full to find any more words to describe what had just happened.

Normally he'd start his leaving routine about now. Faking tiredness, faking a reason to go. Because staying the night, actually sleeping with a woman was a commitment too far that gave too many messages, meant too many things that he did not or could not feel. And, with his head swimming in and out of rationality, distance would have probably been a good thing right now.

Should he leave? How could he leave? A better man would leave when there was no possible future for them. No long-term promises doomed to fail. She was warm, so beautiful. Anchoring him in a place he wanted to stay a while.

An insane man would leave.

Her fingers tiptoed down his chest. 'Oh. I just remembered, you were going to tell me about the scars.'

'Not this again. They are nothing.' His heart began to thud. Not from the memory of the operation—that had been like child's play in comparison—but because of the associations, the ramifications of his time in hospital. But he never talked about this. Especially not after something so intimate that had made him off balance. 'It is time to sleep.'

'Matteo, it's still early. I'm wired...' She shifted over him and he could feel her heart beating against his stomach. Tender kisses across his abdomen.

He gave her backside a gentle tap and tried to play, to distract her from what felt like her only conversation choice. 'You know, you have a peachy bum too, Miss Leigh. Maybe we could do his and hers calendars. That would raise a bit of money for the hospital.'

'Matteo! That's hysterical. It would raise a lot of eyebrows, and knowing the board it would probably lose me my job. If I don't lose it anyway when I don't turn up for work on Monday.'

A tremor of irritation rippled through him. It was supposed to have been a joke. 'Always your job…it's like it's the only thing that matters.' He got it. It was what he'd always prided himself on too. But now…?

No. Now it was still the same. Nothing had changed. He was still the same Matteo, she was still the hospital lawyer who he happened to be in bed with. Nothing more.

At least, that was what he was trying to convince himself.

She gave him a confused look. 'It's not the only thing that's important. Surely you know that about me now? I'm here, aren't I? I mean…here, for my mum, of course.' Her eyes had flitted away from his face and he had no idea what she was think-ing—perhaps, like him, she was surprised at how quickly things had moved from the pub to the bed. The intensity of emotions.

She ran fingertips across the top of his pubic bone. Her voice had been serious for a moment, but now it was lighter. 'So, you have four laparos-copy scars and a longer one here, stretching across your abdomen. That looks…' Levering herself up onto one elbow, she looked straight at him. 'Wait a minute…am I right? Did you…no? Matteo? Did you donate one of your kidneys?'

That was so obvious he couldn't lie. 'Elemen-tary, Miss Leigh. You can be my number-one stu-dent. So don't ever ask me to give you a kidney, because now I don't have any to spare.'

'But why?' Her eyes darkened. A stormy sea. 'Who did you give it to? Wait…let me guess. Oh, my God. It was you. You gave the kidney to your sister?'

'Very good.'

She jerked upright, grasping the sheet and wrap-ping it round her breasts. It looked like she was settling in for a long talk. 'You donated your kid-ney. My God, when? How old were you?'

He didn't need to lay his life out to her. But he knew she would not stop asking. And this one act he had done he was proud of. 'Eighteen. It was one of the first laparoscopic transplants in Milan.'

'You saved her life.'

Not wanting to see any more questions in Ivy's eyes, he laid his head on her lap and looked up at the ceiling. 'I gave her more time. Transplants can last for ten, twenty years. Sometimes up to forty—after that we just don't know.'

'Wow. You must have been such a hero to your family.'

'It was the easiest decision I've ever had to make. Ever. No one else was such a close match.' That time…those memories. Without being able to control it, the tension rose through him.

She must have sensed it too because her voice lowered, a hand went to his shoulder. 'What? What happened?'

'It is too long ago.'

'Let me see…' Drumming her fingers on his ribcage, she thought for a few minutes. 'Your sister…and… It's something to do with your father. Let's examine the evidence.'

Per l'amor di Dio. It was so long ago and yet

the pain still lingered—not overtly but under the surface. A stark reminder of why he never trusted his heart to anyone. Why he never could.

Ivy needed to know that, especially now. 'Okay. Okay. I was engaged to be married. Elizabetta. She lived in the same village as me. Her family were like our family too. We grew up together. We fell in love at eight years old. Our lives were planned in the cradle.'

'What has this got to do with these?' She popped a finger into the dip of each of the faded round scars. 'I don't understand.'

'We…we were always "we" from as far back as I can remember. We had plans—big plans—fuelled by my father, who saw the village as a tie and the restaurant as a failing burden with no future. He filled our heads with dreams, to go to Florence to study medicine, to conquer the world. So that was my life. Study. Working in the restaurant. Elizabetta. It was all leading up to us escaping the small closed-in village and exploring the world.'

Ivy looked at him as if she'd never had those kinds of dreams. Then he realised that escape for her had meant just getting out of hospital. Escape had meant being able to put one foot in front of the other. Escape was knowing there was someone who cared about her enough to help her fight the injustices she'd faced.

Maybe if he'd narrowed his world down to such singular things then he wouldn't have run the risk he had. But he'd had no choice in the end.

'Then my sister got sick. It was sudden and irreversible and she was going to die without a transplant. Dialysis could only help her for so long. We were all tested and I was the lucky one who went off to Milan with her and we had more tests and were away for a few weeks with sporadic contact with our families.' He gave a hollow laugh. 'Who knows, if we'd had your fabulous social media back then, things might have been different.'

He felt Ivy's quiet laugh against his chest.

If things had been different he wouldn't be here, doing this. He wouldn't have found her. A twist of fate that meant his life was more now, richer.

'When we eventually came home Elizabetta had changed. She was quiet and distant—one minute she was loving, the next she couldn't bear to look at me. Eventually she told me she was pregnant. That she had to stay in the village, that we had to change our plans. So I…what do you say?….*sucked* it up. I put my plans aside. I stopped studying. I missed the start of the medical school course. I started to build a life there, working for my father—who berated me every day for giving up on my dream so easily. For not escaping as he'd wanted to do. He laughed at me. Said I should go far away and take Elizabetta with me.'

'Easy for him to say.'

But hard to watch his son throw his life away, Matteo guessed. Hindsight was a wonderful thing. How would he have reacted if he'd watched his son give up his dreams? 'I had made the same mistake he had—got a girl pregnant—and he could see the same pattern happening. He was angry and disappointed. And so, deep down, was I. Everything started to crowd into my head. It was a dark time. I had no future that I wanted and a fiancée who hardly spoke to me. But I tried to make the best of it and grew to love the child inside the woman I wasn't sure loved me any more. This was my problem and I was dealing with it.'

She had started to stroke his hair. It was comforting. Sweet. 'Big decisions at such a young age.'

And he'd thought himself such a man. How

wrong he'd been. 'One day I was out walking, trying to piece my life together, when I caught her and Rafaele together in the fields. Something they'd apparently been doing since I'd gone to Milan. And probably before.'

'Rafaele?'

'A friend.' He could barely even say the word because it did not describe how Matteo felt about Rafaele. Not at all. 'When I confronted them Elizabetta admitted she loved us both, that she was torn between us. And that she hadn't known how to tell me. That the baby I'd given my future up for wasn't even mine. Rafaele just stood there. Silent. He had nothing to say.'

'What did you do?'

Matteo shrugged. 'She'd lied to me. He'd lied to me, too, and there he was, not defending himself. Not saying anything. He had insulted me and any honour or pride I had. So I hit him. Then I told Elizabetta that I would make the decision easy for her and went to pack my things. Back at the house my father laughed in my face. Told me I'd been taken for a ride, that I'd given up my future for nothing. That I was worth nothing. Thank

God I didn't hit him too. But I wanted to. I so very nearly did. In the end I just walked away.'

It was the first time he'd ever spoken about this. It was at once cathartic and yet disturbing to re-live it again. But the anger wasn't as intense as it had been. It felt like the dark stain on his heart had finally begun to fade. Ivy's soothing voice encouraged him to go on. 'I don't blame you. It sounds very messed up.'

'They have four children now. They have the life I had been prepared to have, in the village where we all grew up.'

Ivy's fingers massaged the tops of his shoulders now. 'Which explains why you don't want to go back. I understand now. And why you insist on honesty. Because you had your trust broken com-pletely. I get that. But you have an amazing life now. Look at all the good you do.'

It was, he realised, an empty life that he filled with work. A life like Ivy's. They were the same, the two of them. Trying to convince themselves that they were okay. That they were living just fine. Because that way they didn't have to risk any part of themselves. They were scared, under-neath it all. Scared.

'But it stays with you. Even just a little bit, no matter how much you try to let it all go. Lies can ruin lives. But not as much as love does.'

CHAPTER ELEVEN

Scratch. Scratch. Scratch.

Ivy opened her eyes and tried to work out where the noise was coming from. For that matter, what the noise was. And where the hell *she* was.

Scratch. Meow.

Hugo. Of course. The spare room. With… Wriggling a foot to the other side of the bed, she tested the temperature. Cold. He was long gone. She was in the spare room and *not* with Matteo.

But his scent remained, and, with it the memories of a wonderful night of lovemaking. Of intense emotion. Of discovering that part of him that he held back. The reason he had his famous reputation of non-commitment. It wasn't hard to see why. His history was punctuated with hurt and betrayal and she knew how that felt.

Like right now. When she wanted so much to believe in the fairy-tale ending, and yet he had already disappeared into the night like a guilty gigolo. It would have been nice if he'd had the decency to at least say goodbye. It wasn't as if she hadn't known this would happen, especially after his words last night, but what surprised her was how much it hurt.

Getting out of bed, she pushed the negativity away. It had been a wonderful weekend, and she had begun to feel things she'd never thought possible. She'd laughed and worried and held onto him, exposed her inner fears and experienced such intense joy. He'd made her feel important and special and worthy.

And that, she realised, was the problem.

Downstairs in the kitchen Hugo wound around her feet as if she was the last person alive on earth. In danger of being knocked off balance between her dodgy foot and a starving, needy cat, she picked him up. 'At least someone's pleased to see me.'

Snuggling her face into his fur, she got some comfort from a warm, beating heart under her fingers and the purr that sounded, indeed, like a drill. So what if it was all cupboard love? She was under absolutely no pretences with the cat. Shame she couldn't say the same about her own love life.

And there it was again. That feeling of panic. It wasn't love. It had been one night, the only thing they could ever share. She knew that, they both did. It would be ludicrous to want otherwise.

Plopping Hugo back on the floor, she turned to the fridge. 'Hold on, buster. Here's some food—'

Whoa. A magnet with a pretty terrible amateurish painting of Scarborough beach held a handwritten note on the fridge door:

Ivy
   Joey is sick. I have gone back to London in a hurry. I will phone you.
   Matteo x

She was disappointed at how much her heart soared at those few words. At the hope she imbued into the one tiny letter at the end of the note. What was wrong with her? Instead of worrying about that poor boy, she'd been buoyed by the thought that Matteo had not run away but had left because of an emergency. She'd never been like this before—living in hope of a word, a caress. Been desperate for a man's touch, a kiss. It was infusing everything she did. Infecting her thoughts. Making her feel anxious and excitable.

So being here helping her mum to recuperate had come at the right time. It meant she didn't have to face Matteo right now, she could hunker down and get on top of her wayward emotions, work out a way of avoiding him when she got back, and then she'd back to her normal self.

Talking of which… Ivy glanced at the oven clock. Damn. She was late.

Two hours later she bundled her mum—and Richard, which was a strange turn of events, but, really, not so surprising after all—out of the taxi and back into the house. 'Okay, sit down, Mum, and…er…Richard.'

'Thank you, Ivy. Shoo. Shoo.' Richard pushed Hugo roughly from the sofa, sat down and got a hiss in return. 'Oh, and, please, you can call me—'

'Right. Okay…so…' *Please, don't do that* you can call me dad *routine.* She'd been through too many dads all in all. And they had all turned out like her real one—absent. Picking up Hugo, she gave him a conciliatory stroke. 'I'll pop the kettle on, make a pot of tea and start on lunch.'

Angela gave her a weary smile that was irritated

or exasperated or something that Ivy couldn't put her finger on. But was all too familiar. 'That's very kind of you, darling, especially when I know how much you need to be getting back to your important job. Are you packed yet? What time's the train? Should we call you a taxi?'

What? Train? Taxi? 'I was going to stay a few days, make sure you're okay. You know, like we agreed.' *Mum and daughter time.* 'I want to make sure you're okay.' *That we're okay.*

'Oh, don't worry about that. Richard said he'd cook me dinner tonight, and he's going to pop in every day to check up on me.' Her mother reached out and gave Richard's hand a squeeze, and then left her hand there, tight in his fist, and they looked comfortable and settled—how had they done that in such a short space of time? How had they given themselves up to this, whatever it was. For as long as it lasted. 'Every day, he says. So I'll be fine. Don't feel like you have to stay on my account. We'll be just fine.'

'Oh. Of course, yes, I see.' Ivy didn't know what else to say as she turned away. But she could see very clearly that she wasn't any use now. Richard was going to fill the hole in her mother's life,

Ivy could go back to her job, to her other life in London with no need to worry. Except she'd so wanted to fix things with her mum now she was here.

But she didn't want to do it with an audience, and she knew it would need a lot more than the few precious minutes they had right now—and with a mother who had a focus on that and not on another potential husband.

It was yet another example of her mum's erratic behaviour. Her short attention span where Ivy was concerned. And, yes, it hurt.

Damn it, don't cry. She squeezed her eyelids shut and forced back any sign of distress. Maybe leaving was for the best.

She looked back over at her mum and had to admit she did look happy and relaxed, and the best she'd been since her heart scare. Ivy caught a smattering of her conversation with Richard. 'Stay right there,' he was saying in a quietly calm voice. 'I'll get a cushion for you. Wait…wait…I want to make sure you're comfortable.'

The man was certainly attentive, even if he didn't appear to like cats. And who was she to deprive her mum of some happiness? If she'd been suffering from depression for all those years and now she wasn't—if this man made her happy and this was what Angela wanted, then she had to let it go. Regardless of her own misgivings.

'I don't know,' her mother replied, looking up at her new man with a sort of adoration as he plumped a cushion and fussed around her. 'You and your fussing ways, you'll drive me crazy.'

'You'll get used to it. See that my way is best.' Richard gave her mum a smile and Ivy's heart lurched.

You drive me crazy.

They were only words. But she'd used them to Matteo and he'd used them right back. And it was the sentiment, it was the same—you drive me crazy, but that's okay. What's a bit of madness between friends? Losing sanity. It was two people becoming a little less of who they were for the sake of someone else. It was Ivy becoming Angela.

Her hand went to her mouth. Oh, my goodness. Of all the things she'd dreaded. She couldn't let that happen.

But it was too late, Ivy *was* different. He had made her different, he'd made her yearn for more.

For more in her life than just work. Which was impossible. Just downright impossible, if she was going to be true to her herself and her years of promises and grit.

If she went back to London tonight she would have to face Matteo again too soon and she didn't know what she would say, or how to act, or how to be the same person she'd been before. Before she'd ever met him.

Truth was, she wasn't sure of anything any more. Of where she fitted in her own life, or in other people's. Fighting back the sting of more tears, she walked into the kitchen. At that same moment her phone rang. She pulled it out of her pocket, unable to see the number for the teary blur, which she scrubbed away as quickly as it arrived.

There was absolutely no point in getting emotional about any of this. She just needed to compartmentalise her feelings and move on, like she always did. 'Hello?'

'Ivy?'

Matteo. She swallowed back the lump in her throat and disregarded the accompanying jittery heart rate at the sound of his voice. She would not show him any reason to feel sorry for her, she would not let him know her feelings. She infused her voice with cheeriness. 'Hello! How's Joey?'

'Good, you saw the note. He's a lot better now. He had a ureteral obstruction, which didn't resolve with a nephrostomy. I operated early this morning.'

'Er…English, Matteo?' Cradling the phone between her ear and her shoulder, she filled the kettle, plonked two teabags into a teapot and tried very hard to act normally.

'I had to take him back to Theatre to unblock a blockage. What is wrong?'

'Nothing. Nothing at all.'

'But your voice isn't right. You are upset?' He knew the timbre of her voice? He knew her so well he could tell when she was upset, without words? He knew her too well. She'd let him in too—she'd let him in and she was going to get hurt. Because that's what happened if she let her guard down. There was a pause she didn't know how to fill. Then he was back again.

'Are you cross because I left? I'm sorry I had to leave so quickly and so early. I didn't want to wake you.' Another pause, then his voice was more serious. 'I need to talk to you.'

Uh-huh. She knew exactly what was coming, but she couldn't do a heart-to-heart, not without understanding what the heck was going on in her head and why her body had become a quivering mess. Why she desperately needed to feel his arms around her when it was the opposite of what she should be needing.

But something had to be said, surely? They'd moved further into something last night. Something tangible and deep and frighteningly wonderful. And so very, very dangerous. A line had been crossed and it couldn't be ignored.

But it could be delayed. Until she'd got a better grip on herself. 'Another time, Matteo. I'm busy... I have too much to do.'

'That is what I mean.'

'Sorry? You're not making sense.'

'I saw the boss today at the hospital. Pinkney. I told him your dilemma and he agreed to a week of compassionate leave. You can stay with your mum and work can wait. I fixed it for you.' He had a smile in his voice and she imagined that wonderful mouth curving upwards, the light in his eyes. And felt a stab of pain in her solar plexus.

You drive me crazy.

And he did. And that was the problem. He drove her wild with desire, he drove her to the edge, he drove her to want things she couldn't have. To dream impossible things. And now he was trying to fix her messed-up life. And it would be so easy to let him do it—so easy, and yet the hardest thing in the world. Because she could not let go of her grip on her life.

'But, you see…I don't want you to do that. I don't need you to fix things for me, I can manage quite well on my own. I don't need you. I don't need anyone.' It was harsh. And it was everything she needed to believe and feel again but didn't, but if she kept on saying it he'd get the message and she wouldn't have to face him. Or this. Or herself.

'I thought that was what you wanted. I was trying to help.' She could hear the building anger in his voice. And, yes, he'd been kind, as always, and thought he was doing the right thing. But, as it turned out, she hadn't needed him to. Once again she was surplus to Angela's requirements.

'Thank you. But I won't be needing it. Please,

don't interfere in things like that again. Not my work. Thank you.'

'Hey! Stop right there. Do not talk to me as if I am just a colleague, as if there is nothing between us. Ivy, we need to talk.'

'I'm not sure there's anything to say.'

His voice was louder, harsher. 'And I think there is. I think that what happened last night meant something. Did it mean nothing to you?'

She could lie, but he'd know. He *knew* her. He knew what had passed between them last night, the startling honesty and the wonder—that wasn't something she could deny. It had been too profound, too…too *much*—and it had shocked them both. She lowered her voice, the truth of her words like glass shards in her gut. 'Yes. Yes. It meant something.'

'So explain to me what is happening here, because I'm confused. You're distant and different from the woman I know. Damn it, Ivy, tell me the truth.'

I'm saying that you mean too much to me. That I have to let you go. 'I'm sorry, really. I do have to go.' Her heart twisted keenly, making her inhale. But her lungs wouldn't work. She forced the words through a closed throat. 'Goodbye, Matteo.'

It was for the best. It was. And one day she'd thank herself for it.

Without waiting another moment, she flicked the phone off and went up to her room to pack. It was time to go home.

Wherever the hell that was. But it wasn't here. And it wasn't in Matteo's arms.

Round three. Part one.

Matteo circumvented the tasteless coffee table and surreptitiously drank out of his clandestine cup as he mingled with the waiting group. The only saving grace was that Ivy wouldn't be here to tempt him, to confuse him. To drive him mad all over again.

In fact, it was very useful that he'd had to leave in the night to come and see Joey, before he'd had a chance to do anything even more foolish than make love to a woman who was destined to trample all over his heart. She'd proved that enough when she'd answered his attempts at intimacy with silence. Refuted his well-intentioned intervention into her work life—which, for the record, he'd thought was the right thing to do.

But that would never happen again, not if it generated such a response. He could feel his blood pressure rising at the memory of her sharp words and the swiftly ended phone call. The reminder that relationships brought about all kinds of problems that he was better not having.

He took a seat in the front row, glared at the clock. Willed the day to be over so he could get the big fat tick on his attendance sheet and eventually put this whole exercise behind him. Then he wouldn't have any more unreturned calls to Ivy Leigh. Along with the whole bunch of questions and no answers.

The door swung open and her assistant walked in, handed out the day's schedule. And—

In walked Ivy.

Matteo's head pounded. That blood pressure was rising at an alarming rate. Why was she not in York?

'Good morning, everyone.' She was all business and no eye contact. Well, no eye contact with him at any rate. 'Welcome to the third day in our social media course. Today we are going to expand on branding and why it is important in this techno-logical age to capitalise on it. I'm going to give a few pointers about how we do this as a company, and how you can help...'

He didn't want to help. He wanted it to be over. He wanted to be alone with her. He wanted her. That was the startling, raw, naked truth of it. And at the same time he knew that wanting a woman who did not want him back was the first step to madness.

Two hours later they were split into more infu-riating groups to discuss brand statements. Ivy walked over, her limp undiminished—in fact, worse than usual. He put it down to the bicycle accident. She looked tired and frazzled and dis-tant. To stop himself from spending too much time just looking at her, at the proud, straight back, the curve of a breast he knew was lush and sweet, the unintentionally honest green eyes, he started to give his ideas to the group. 'Brand state-ments... Okay. We help children. We save lives. I know...we save children's lives...er... Children first? Kids first...? *Aargh.* This is pointless. I'm a doctor, not a marketing person. I instinctively know what the brand is, I live the damned thing every day—why do I have to come up with a statement?'

She stopped at his shoulder. 'So that we are all on the same page, Mr Finelli. If we have a mission statement and a brand statement that are symbiotic then we all have a pathway for our work.'

Mr Finelli now, was it? 'I already have one and, I imagine, so does everyone here. It's about doing our best…for everyone. And about being *open* and *honest* about intention.'

Judging by the two hot spots on her cheeks, she took the veiled meaning for what it was. He didn't like playing guessing games. He didn't like hot and cold. He liked to know exactly where he stood. On all things. He didn't like having the phone put down on him when he was trying hard to work things through.

'I…I…understand…' She looked away. 'So—'

'I am not sure you do, Miss Leigh. This hospital is about children, we all know that. Children are not a brand, they are people. Living, breathing, vulnerable and sick people. Show me how branding can really, actually, honestly change a single life more than what we do here every day then I'll be impressed. Until then, well, I just want to do my job in peace. Like you, I presume, with no needless distractions.'

For a moment she stared at him open-mouthed, the two hot-spots spreading across her neck like a rash. And he immediately regretted allowing his frustration to overspill into this public domain.

She gave a quick clap of her hands. 'Okay, everyone, let's break for morning tea.' Then she turned to him and whispered, 'Outside. Now.'

A cruel wind whipped at the side of the red-brick hospital building as they huddled in a disused doorway. She'd made sure they were well away from prying ears and eyes. So typical. Anything to keep the work-life divide real. He cut through the tension. 'Ivy. How come you are here? Your mum?'

'Is fine, it appears. I came back on Sunday. The train...' Her tone was dismissive, not allowing for any more discussion on that subject. 'It's not important.'

'I see.' This was a surprise, especially given the compassionate leave she'd been granted and her stated intention that she wanted to fix things. She clearly wasn't going to expand on this, she was closed off and wound as tight as that first day he'd met her. Was this really the warm-hearted woman who had held him so tightly outside the cardiac care unit? Who had screamed loudly in a pub? Who had laughed heartily at his jokes? Who had gripped him and exposed her fears? Who had lain breathless and spent on his bed after the best lovemaking of his life?

She looked at him now with a taut line of a mouth. With eyes that she clearly hoped were cold and distant but which gave away a traitorous flicker of heat. She would not like to know that, he supposed. 'So work won out in the end? I'm surprised, Ivy. I thought you had changed your priorities a little. What do you want to say to me?'

'Work did not win. My mother simply didn't need me.' That flicker of heat gave way to sadness. Something had happened between her and her mum and she was dealing with it badly. 'Now, I'd be grateful if you could keep our personal life out of the work environment.'

'Since when did I bring it in?'

Her eyes fired up again. 'When you spoke to Pinkney. And with the between-the-lines comments in there. I'm at work. We both are. Please, remember that.'

Leaning against the wall, he looked at her, barely trying to disguise his surprise and growing anger. 'No one knows anything. And since you have refused to speak to me in private I'm stuck with having to put things between the lines. I told you about my life, I told you how much I value honesty. What the hell is going on, Ivy?'

'I...' She shook her head, the tautness of her mouth softening, wobbling slightly, and for a moment he thought she might cry. 'I don't know what to say. Just that I'm sorry, but...'

And it was all well and good being angry with her, but he knew deep down that she was not a hurtful kind of woman. That she was facing challenges that were testing her, pushing her to the limits. That she was warm and funny and with a lot to give and usually had too many words but now had none.

Matteo stepped closer but ignored the need to pull her to him. She was so proud she would never allow that. He kept his voice low. 'Okay. Talk to me. Please, that's all I ask. I will start. This all took me by surprise. Things went from slow to fast in a heartbe—'

'Yes. Yes.' She held her hand up and stopped

him from saying more. 'Thank goodness you feel the same. Too fast, Matteo. Too deep. Too quick. I never wanted this. I like being on my own. I like not having to make decisions for someone else. I'm too independent for all this. Last weekend was…nice. And thank you. But we can't… I can't—'

'Nice? Nice? All the words in the world and that's the one you choose. Oh, Ivy. What kind of game are you playing? Because I don't understand your rules. One day you were happy to be with me, and now…this coldness.'

'I'm not playing a game. I'm being serious. I don't want a relationship. I can't…do it. I can't give myself…I don't want to.' She looked down at her watch. 'Damn. Look, I have to go back in and start.'

'Just like that, it is over?'

'Yes. Yes, it is.'

He waited for relief to flood in, but it didn't. Only bitter sadness, a hole in his chest. Which was surprising and startling and bleak. The thought that he'd see her over and over again in the hospital and never get to kiss those lips. To hold her close and stroke her cheek. To be at the end of a smart quip. This was not how he'd envisioned he would feel and he didn't know what to do or say. He was out of his depth here, with feelings swirling inside him. He didn't want them but he couldn't seem to let them go. What did it mean?

Did he love her? Surely he could not have done such a thing? He had always protected himself from that. Because of the pain. Because of Elizabetta, because he had been so wary to give his heart to a woman and watch her toss it aside. Was Ivy any different from that? He'd hoped so, but now he wasn't so sure.

'No more talking about it? I have no choice?'

'No. Please. Don't make me say anything else. Because I don't know what more to say.' She gave a swift shrug of her shoulder and blinked away what he thought might be tears. 'I really do have to go and finish this workshop.'

'Always your job.'

'Oh, yes, well, you know me. No hard feelings?'

'I thought I did know you, but I was wrong.' He watched as she swivelled on the hard gravel and began to walk back towards the conference room. 'And, no, Ivy, I have no hard feelings. I have no feelings about this at all.'

And that was when he knew that he'd fallen completely for her. That he had given her much, much more than he'd ever intended; he'd given her his heart on a platter and all but invited her to chop it into pieces. Yes, he knew he'd fallen in too deep, because saying he had no feelings was the first real lie he'd ever told.

CHAPTER TWELVE

'BACK FOR MORE, I see? You're a glutton for punishment.' Nancy gave Ivy a little smile as she gave her wet hands a shake and scanned the OR prep-room sinks, looking for the paper towels. 'You've done so well, considering what you were like that first time.'

'Thanks.' It was all Ivy could muster. She was feeling much worse than that first day—she may well have mastered the sight of blood, but mastering the sight of Matteo Finelli was something she would probably never be able to do. She could see him through the glass door in the OR, talking and laughing with the anaesthetist. Her stomach clenched into a tight ball.

She didn't want to face him today, because yesterday she'd felt as if her heart was shattering. She'd summoned every single ounce of strength she'd had to tell him it was over, when it felt like the words had been stuck in her throat, refusing to come out. She'd had no sleep, curled up with Hugo, who she'd rescued from the clutches of *daddy Richard*. And, unsurprisingly, Hugo had been about as helpful with relationship advice as her mother.

And now…well, now she had to stand with Matteo all day and watch him save another life. Watch him laugh and joke and be lovely and warm to all those people and feel her heart beating to the rhythm of his voice, feel the pull of her body towards him, and know that it made no sense to take those steps, no matter how much she was compelled to.

The door swung open and he strode in.

Looking around, she realised Nancy had gone and they were alone. She took a deep breath. 'Matteo, hello.'

'I thought it was Mr Finelli these days.' He wasn't wearing a surgical mask so she felt the full effect of his indifference. No, actually, it was a simmering deep anger that he'd dressed up as indifference. She'd hurt him and that had not been her intention.

'Matteo, please—'

He shook his head. 'Miss Leigh, I can honestly

say that I have no problem whatsoever about bow-
ing out of our petty little war. I'm even happy to
admit you to be the winner—in truth, it makes no
difference to me. So you have no need to be here.'
He came a little closer, not close enough that she
could touch him but enough that she felt the mag-
netic pull towards him, and feel, too, the venom
in his words. 'In fact, I'm asking you leave.'

'To leave? But—why?'

His eyes bored into her, stern, angry, righteous.
'Because having you here distracts me. I need to
be fully focused on my work. It is better if you're
not here, particularly for the patient. And that,
after all, is the full focus of *your* job, right?'

'Matteo, please—'

This time he held up his hand and she shut up
immediately. 'Did you really think I would let you
in? What an idea! When you don't let anyone in
yourself? When you don't even know how?'

'I can't. I tried, but I can't.' Because the second
she'd let him in she'd started to be someone else.
She hadn't been Ivy Leigh any more…and she
didn't want that. She wanted to keep herself intact.

'Things might have worked if we'd both wanted
to try.'

'But…' She finally found the words to admit how she was feeling. 'I don't want to lose myself.'

'I know. I understand that. Who does? Have you ever thought that perhaps, just perhaps, we could have had a…what did you call it?…symbiotic pathway? Walk it together? Be ourselves and yet part of something?'

She thought of her mum and her flatmate and of the weekend and of how desperately she'd ached for Matteo when he hadn't been there. How he had become the focus of her thoughts. 'Everything I've ever seen has shown me that independence becomes interdependence and then dependence. I don't want to depend on anyone. That wouldn't be me. I don't want to be like that.'

He huffed out an exasperated breath. 'It doesn't have to be like that. I know plenty of people who have managed to have happy relationships. You don't even want to take the risk.'

Please, don't ask again. Because I might just say yes. 'No, Matteo. I don't. For both of our sakes. It wouldn't be fair.' She turned away from him, unable to keep looking at those dark eyes that drew her in so deep. 'Okay. I'll go, if you insist. But I won't say I've won. I don't even want to think about that.' This was no victory at all. 'I think we've both won. And lost. And now I'm talking in circles. I'll just go.'

'Yes. Please.'

She went to leave, biting back the shout, *I want you. Please, don't do this.* Fighting back tears, knowing that stopping this before it became too intense, too hard to handle, too overpowering was the very right thing to do, even though her heart told her otherwise. But she hadn't achieved all those amazing things in her life by listening to her heart. So it had no right to interfere now.

Her head bobbed a little as she leaned towards the door. She was going.

'Ivy. Stop.' Matteo felt the blood boiling through his veins. This was not the best way to start a difficult day in the OR. This was not how he had planned this conversation to go. He had been going to ban her from the theatre, yes, but he hadn't wanted to see her look so accepting of his rejection. So vulnerable. 'This...this is... Just listen, you're making me say things I don't mean. You're making me crazy.'

She turned a little, her eyes brighter. Her mouth made a tentative attempt at a smile, but it just looked sad. 'I know, and that's the biggest problem of all. Apparently it doesn't get any better with age. So my mum says, and she should know.'

'She is better now?'

'She's exactly the same as always. With a slightly damaged heart. But haven't we all?'

He laughed. He actually laughed. Right in the middle of this…break-up of something that wasn't even a whole of anything. He laughed. Because she was impressive, this woman. She was more than impressive. She had shown up today knowing that it would be the hardest thing to face him, but she had done it anyway. She had kept her sorrows to herself. She had hidden her emotions and kept on working. It was either admirable or downright destructive. Or both.

And no matter what words came out of his mouth the feelings remained the same. He was awash with anger at her decision, with joy at knowing the real woman underneath the hard veneer, with a frustration that she was so damned private. With pride that she'd chosen him to take to bed, to tell her secrets to when she'd been ready. With a yearning for more and more and more, and he didn't know what any of that meant.

And then he did. The pieces began to slip into place.

He had fallen in love with her. Of all the women in the damned hospital, in the damned city, in the whole damned world to fall in love with, he had chosen the most complicated, stubborn, uptight one of all. And now she was walking away and there was nothing he could do or say to make her stop because she didn't believe she could do it. She didn't believe that love could happen for her.

And so this was what he was left with: he loved her and he didn't know what to do with it. He didn't want to love her. He didn't want to like her even. Because, *oh, mio Dio,* she could be very difficult and all she cared about was her work.

Like him. Like he used to be.

He turned away and tried to steady himself. Panic swirled in his gut. He had protected himself for years against this. But, it seemed, it was something you could not fight in the end.

'*Ciao*, Matteo. And thank you for everything. It was a hell of a lot better than nice.' She was going. Leaving, because he had made her go. His mind began to swirl too. Why this? Why now? Why, in hell, *her*? But the only answers were right in front of his eyes.

'Wait.'

Taking too many steps closer to her, he touched her cheek. Pulled her to him. And he felt hesitation. For a moment he thought she might push him away, but instead she dragged him to her, clamped her mouth hard against his.

'Matteo…'

She was in his arms and the emotions filled his chest thick and heavy and yet weightless, and he tried to hold them back but they just kept coming, rising and filling him with this urgent need. 'Ivy, *ti amo*.'

And he hoped she did not understand or hear him, because the moment he'd said those words he'd known it was the wrong thing to say. The last thing he should do was open his heart to her.

Then he was kissing her again. A rough, hard kiss filled with every damned ounce of emotion he had in him, and she was kissing him back with just as much. With anger. With joy and frustration that they just wouldn't work, because she didn't want them to.

And because that had been the one startlingly honest thing she had said, he kissed her some more.

'Okay, people, let's get going. Oh. God. Sorry. Oops. Bad timing.'

It was Nancy. Matteo winced. Now, to add humiliation to Ivy's list of worries, their privately public display would definitely be hospital gossip.

Ivy jerked away, the space where she'd been in his arms now just a heavy emptiness. She was swiping her hand across her mouth. Then she was gone. Along with his hope.

He looked around for something to kick, to hit, to assuage these feelings of hurt and anger and…this new feeling of love. But there was a surge of people into the adjoining room. A child who needed an operation. A family waiting for his skills. A team needing to be led. So he just balled his hands into fists and took a minute to let the emotions wash through him.

His heart was as empty as his arms. Because he knew, with certainty, that she would never come back. That he had lost her. Because she had never known such a thing as love and she was so desperately in need of it but, oh, so afraid. And now he had lost it too.

* * *

'Well done. You were great in there! Scary, but great.' Becca gave Ivy a high five as they walked away from the sexual harassment tribunal. The wind had dropped and the afternoon was promising to be unseasonably warm. They took the shortcut through Regent's Park back towards the hospital, dodging what appeared to be some kind of kiddie fun run event as they walked. 'You knew exactly what you were doing, and you wiped the floor with his defence.'

Ivy smiled. Ah, the naivety of the inexperienced. 'I just let the evidence speak for itself. There really wasn't anything he could say in the face of three witnesses.' But Becca was right. She had felt like a fight this morning. In fact, she had felt like a fight quite a lot recently. She put it down to lack of sleep. Which in turn was a result of… She wouldn't think about it. She wouldn't think about him any more. It was too exhausting. Too damaging to ache and want and dream, and need someone so badly. She just needed to focus on work some more and he'd be gone from her brain soon. He would.

The trouble was, almost a week on and he was still there, looming large inside her head.

'But you just kept on. You were epic. I started to feel a bit sorry for him by the end. You needled and needled until he admitted everything.' Becca put her hand on Ivy's arm. 'Girl crush alert. I think I'd like to be you when I grow up.'

'Oh, no, you wouldn't. Believe me. I do everything wrong.'

Becca shook her head. 'What? You just won a case, you did that right. You want to celebrate?' They'd stopped outside a café, the smell of strong dark coffee irresistible. And, for some reason, Ivy felt like staying a while, not rushing back. The thought of her stuffy office was nothing compared to the fresh air, the kids' squeals and cheers as they crossed the finishing line. Ivy envied them their innocence.

'Okay. A quick one.'

Ivy placed the order and found Becca sitting at an outside table, swatting a large bee away. 'I asked them to be quick. Shouldn't be too long.'

'Doesn't matter if it is. To be honest, with the hours you've put in this week you're owed a small break and... Oh, don't they look pretty? So fresh and gorgeous.' Becca was pointing towards a carpet of red and white flowers. 'Tulips? I never know the names of flowers.'

Ivy pulled out her notepad. 'So, about tomorrow's course. Are you sure you can handle it? You know the schedule?'

Becca rolled her eyes. 'We've been over and over this. Yes, I can handle it. It's only the wrap-up, question time and feedback. It won't be hard. But, you know, I did just point out that absolutely stunning tulip bed over there, and can you smell that divine smell? There are some seriously beautiful plants here but you don't appear to notice them. Or anything out of the confines of your office.'

Becca inhaled and looked a little apprehensive. 'I wasn't going to say anything, but I can't let you go on like this. I know you're not running tomorrow's social media course because Dr Peachy Bum will be there…but I don't know why. What on earth happened?'

'Becca. Please.' Ivy didn't need this. She was coping just fine, and would continue to do so as long as she didn't have to speak about it. Or think about him. 'I have an unavoidable meeting with the board tomorrow, you know that.'

'You could have rearranged it. Said you had an important previous appointment. And, yes, I'm overstepping again, but I'm worried about you. Seriously. You've been head down all week, locked in your office until all hours—and I know you think we all believe you're working, but I can see straight through you. There's not much more done than this time last week.'

'There is. I would never let anything interfere with my work.' Had she? Had she spent time staring out the window? Yes. But that had been critical thinking time. Had she thought about Matteo at all?

Okay, yes. She'd thought about little else. She missed him. Missed having his arms wrapped around her, missed feeling able to tell him anything. Missed his smile and his laugh and...okay, yes. She missed his bum too.

Becca tapped her finger on the tabletop. 'Besides, there are doodles...incriminating doodles...'

'What?'

'In your bin. Words, doodles, hearts. Tearstained hearts…'

And Ivy had thought she'd managed to hide them away at the bottom of the rubbish bin. Hearts. Yeah, right. It was all fluff and nonsense and wishful thinking. 'You are seriously deranged. Either that or you'll go far in this profession—observation and attention to detail are key.' For a moment Ivy thought Becca might explode with such an admission of excited suspicion. 'But sorry to disappoint you, there weren't any tears, I just spilled my water—'

Becca's voice dropped and softened. 'Something happened, something momentous, and you think you can hide it all. But you can't. Guess what? You're human, Ivy, and you're allowed to bleed.'

Sure, but what if it never stops? 'It wasn't… I didn't…'

'What happened?'

'Nothing.'

The coffee came and it was satisfactory, but not as nice as the one Matteo had bought for her that day he'd kissed her in the staffroom. Seemed she couldn't do the most mundane of things without thinking about him. *Fade, please, memory. Fade.*

But it didn't fade, it just sent shooting pains to her chest instead. 'I can't talk about it.'

Replacing her cup in its saucer, Becca shook her head. 'Okay. Fine. Spend all your days solving everyone else's problems just so you don't have to think about your own.'

Like her mother? 'That's not why I do this job.'

Her assistant's eyebrows rose. 'Really?'

'No. I do it because I want everyone to get a fair go. I love this job.' Although recently it hadn't held her attention quite as much as it always had. And she knew the reason. She just wasn't ready to admit it. She wanted more in her life than files and injunctions and other people's messes. She wanted a chance at her own happy mess. Hugo had filled a little space, but she ached for more.

For Matteo.

Becca ran her finger round the froth in her cup and licked. 'You love being needed here. Does it…does it stop you from needing something else? Love? A peachy—?'

'Stop it. I should fire you for insubordination.'

'Well, you could, but that would mean you'd have to do tomorrow's course on your own.'

Panic twisted in her stomach. 'I can't see him, Becca. I just can't.'

Becca breathed out and smiled reassuringly. 'Sure you can.'

'I can?' Yes, of course she could. He was just a man. She was fine. 'I don't think I can.'

'So you had a thing?'

Oh, what was the point in denying it? She knew any secrets shared would stay with Becca. She shrugged. 'A small one.'

'Wait, though, you look crushed. You've been so hyped up recently. Oh, Ivy…it wasn't small at all. Was it? Not for you.' Her hand slid across the table to Ivy's shaking one. 'You've fallen in love with him?'

Do not cry. Do not cry. Do not cry. 'I haven't got time to do anything like that. I have a busy job—'

'You do. You love him.'

'And there are a lot of long hours involved. I have to review all the employment contracts starting from next Monday—'

Becca patted her hand. 'It's okay, you know. It's okay to be frightened. It's okay to meet someone halfway. You don't have to give all this up. You can do both. People do both.'

'And then…' Ivy stopped talking. Simply because there was a rock in her throat that she couldn't squeeze words past. But she thought about her life. How she'd been forging forward her whole life because she so wanted people to take her seriously. Wanted people to notice her for the right reasons, and not because she couldn't walk properly. And he had. Matteo had plucked her from the three billion women on the planet and had made her feel important. He'd given her the one thing she'd craved all her life. And it scared her so much. That responsibility, just taking what he was offering, it was overwhelming… Man, she was so scared. 'Yes.'

'Yes, what?'

And she thought about her sleepless nights, and about how much she missed him. How she had never wanted to believe all that *you complete me* guff, but she could see how it could be possible that one person could make you more whole, better, stronger than before. That plenty of people weren't like her mum, plenty of people had happy stable lives that they shared very successfully. It was a question of finding the right person for you.

That person was Matteo. Her heart softened a little at the thought of him. And then filled with panic at the thought that she'd lost him already. 'Yes. I think I love him. I don't know for sure, but I think I could. I'd like to try.' And that scared her the most.

'Hallelujah. Great. Finally, we have a break-through.' Becca raised her hands to the sky and cheered. 'But does he love you back?'

'I sincerely doubt it after everything I've said and done to stop that happening. He thinks I'm selfish and self-centred and only think about my work.'

'Hmm, clearly the man's a good judge of charac-ter.' Becca flashed a smile. 'Seriously, though, did he ever do anything that might make you think he felt the same?'

Ivy thought about the kisses and the night of lovemaking, and driving her all that way home in the rain, and just the simple, sweet look in his eyes when he talked to her. The kisses, though—they couldn't lie about the way he felt. No one could kiss like that and not mean it. 'Yes. Lots and lots.'

'So show him that you're all of those things and so much more. You're driven and dedicated and passionate. Italians like that.'

'He does.' And for the first time in for ever Ivy began to feel a little glimmer of hope blooming in her chest. She breathed deeply, the gorgeous scent of some exotic plant catching in her throat. He was right, there was so much more to life than work. There was him, Matteo Finelli. And her, Poison Ivy. Maybe they could try to be part of something. Something together. 'But I really messed up. I just need to find a way to convince him.'

Becca punched the air. 'Yes! If anyone can, you can. Why don't you just march right up to him and tell him?'

Because she wasn't that brave. 'Because he's the kind of man who judges by actions. I know him, Becca, he's tired of all my words. He was hurt badly once by a girl who said she loved him but acted otherwise. She broke his heart and he's waited all this time to take a chance on someone else. And when he did it backfired and he's re-treated to lick his wounds. It's enough for me to accept that I love him, but I need to work out a way to prove it to him.'

CHAPTER THIRTEEN

IT WAS LATE. The transplant he'd just finished on a thirteen-year-old girl had been very difficult but she was recovering well. He had pre-op blood results to go through for the list tomorrow and an informal ward round to complete. He had a headache. And heartache. And he wanted to go to bed.

But to top off the day from hell, someone had organised a night walk through Regent's Park to raise money for the department. Tonight. For a dialysis machine. So he was duty bound to attend.

'Wow, what's happening?' Regent's Park was one of his usual running spots but as he approached it he was surprised at the size of the crowd. Everywhere he looked he saw people; adults, kids, baby strollers, all dressed up in green, a surging emerald sea. Getting closer, he heard clapping start. Quietly at first, but with every step he took it got louder and louder. And then he began to recognise faces. Joey's mum and dad. Portia, who he'd operated on last year, and her family. Mathilde. Ahmed. Benjamin. All these familiar faces greeting him with cheers and smiles. What the hell? Why were they clapping?

Confused and a little humbled, he stopped at the first marquee with a banner reading *'KIDney Kidz—Give a little, save a life.'* He spoke to a nurse from the intensive care unit. 'Hi. I'm Matteo. I need to pay for my ticket. I think I'm a little late. Where's the start?'

She beamed at him. 'Hi, yes, I know who you are. I think everyone does.'

That damned picture again. 'But—'

'Thanks for everything you've done.' She gave a quick nod. 'We're five minutes away from starting—the line's over there.' She pointed down the crowd of people to the right. 'And it's okay, VIPs don't have to pay.'

VIPs? Now he was really confused. Was this another unfunny Ged joke? 'It's for a good cause. I'd like to give something—'

'I think you've given enough, Matteo.'

He froze. That voice. The northern accent. *Ivy.* His heart thumped. Would it ever stop its Pavlovian response to her? Four weeks and he'd managed to keep out of her way. Four long weeks of hell wondering how to fix something that appeared irrevocably broken.

Sucking in a deep breath, he turned. She was dressed in a green T-shirt and shorts, her hair covered by a green baseball cap. She wore a tentative smile. In her hands she had a clipboard and a large net bag stuffed with green fabric. It was good to see her. Good and bad as his gut tumbled over and over. 'Ivy. What are you doing here?'

Her pretty smile faded. 'A fun run, obviously.'

His gaze flitted from that beautiful, heart-breaking mouth to her leg. 'But your foot?'

'Will be fine, I'm sure. It's only ten kilometres.' Although she looked more defiant than convinced. He had no doubt that if anyone would do it, she would. 'Good turnout.'

'I've never seen so many people at one of our events before. It's miraculous.'

Her head dipped a little as she replied, 'No, Matteo. It's called using the internet for what it's good at.'

'You? You did this?' *What the hell is going on?* 'Yes.'

'How?' *Why?* For some reason his voice was croaky, his throat blocked.

Hers clearly wasn't. She was determined and forthright. Vibrant in her passion for what she'd done. 'I sent out a call. I contacted Joey's mum and dad, who are part of the kidney kids support network, who in turn contacted your previous patients, who promoted the idea on all their social network sites. Within twenty-four hours the buzz got picked up by a radio station. That got covered by the local newspaper. That was online and got clicked on by hundreds of people. Like your bottom, my call went viral. It doesn't happen every time, but this seems to have captured people's imaginations. Your patients and their families wanted to do this, for you. Because of what you'd done for them.'

Whoa. That was humbling and affirming at the same time. 'What was your message?'

'I said...and please don't be angry because only you and I really know what happened...' From her clipboard she peeled off a leaflet with his photo on it. His work profile one, not the one in the locker room. Thank goodness for small mercies. 'Dr Matteo gave the gift of life, now you can too.

One step at a time. Join us on a night walk. Wear green to be seen. KIDney Kidz: We won't fail them.'

'You make me sound too perfect.'

She grinned and her green eyes shone with a fire he'd only seen once before. When he'd been in bed with her. *Mio Dio*, she was beautiful. She'd broken what had been left of his heart—he understood that now. 'Nah—you're just the pretty face poster-boy. Amazing what you can do, even with clothes on. I thought that there must be a lot of people out there who want to show their thanks, and who want to help others in the same situation. It's amazing how many people said yes as soon as your name was mentioned. You have quite a fan club.'

But the one person he wanted wasn't a member. 'I don't know what to say.'

'"Thank you" will suffice. Oh, and at three thousand people, ten quid a head, you've pretty much got your dialysis machine.' He followed her, walking slowly towards the start line, and they became engulfed with people on all sides, chatting, cheering, patting him on the back.

He still couldn't believe it. 'And you organised this in four weeks?'

'I pulled a few strings. Someone I was at university with knows someone who could make it happen. Becca helped too. We were stuffing the goody bags at three this morning.' Her face lit up as she looked at all the smiling faces around them. And he could see the tired edges of her face and he longed to touch her, but he wouldn't. 'It was worth every second.'

'But why? Why did you do this?'

She turned to look at him, her eyes misting. 'Because you got to me in the end. I believe you need this equipment. I believe you, Matteo, when you say children are vulnerable and not a brand. I believe in you. And I wanted to show you how using the internet for the right things can really pay off.' A loud crack split the sky. 'Oh. Looks like we're starting. Come on.'

She stuffed a T-shirt—green, of course—into his hand and started to walk along the path. If her ankle was hurting she certainly had no intention of showing it. She'd done all this for him? Using her skills and knowledge and pure raw grit.

'No. Stop a minute.' He pulled her off the path

for a moment onto lush, warm grass. 'I was wrong about you. Well, kind of wrong and right at the same time. I suppose I can concede that the internet has its advantages. Look at how many people *you* have helped.'

She shook her head. 'I started to do this for you, Matteo. It would be wrong of me to say otherwise. I wanted to make you happy. But, actually, as the whole thing began to gain traction I got so completely invested in it that I had to make it work. Look at Joey there—you've made such a difference. To all of them.'

What was she saying? That this grand gesture was for him? Why? 'I don't understand you, Ivy. You said it was over. You said you didn't want me. And that's okay. Sad, but okay. We have our own lives.' He didn't want to have this conversation. Enough that it was all over between them, without this prolonged attachment. He watched as people streamed by, green balloons bobbing above their heads in the fading daylight, and felt overwhelming emotion. For them. For this. For him and Ivy. Between them they could have made an excellent team.

But that was useless. She'd been trying to prove

a point that she could use social media for a good cause. This wasn't about them. Or about piecing together a broken heart. 'Thank you for doing this—the department will be grateful. I am grateful. We should be going.'

This was not how Ivy had envisaged things going. She'd thought he would be pleased, thrilled enough that she wouldn't have to completely open herself up to him. That he'd accept this whole night run as a sign of how she felt. Which was… overwhelmed. Just being with him again left her breathless and aching for more. To touch him. To kiss him.

Say it.

Bleed if you have to.

She watched him moving quickly in the crowd. 'Matteo. Stop.' Damn. This had not been such a great idea after all. How to declare yourself in front of three thousand runners? *Really?* She doubled her pace, her leg jarring with every footfall, but, damn it, she was going to get through to him, all ten kilometres if she had to—shouting his name all the damned way. 'Matteo! Stop.' He did, finally. 'What I'm trying to say…badly…is that I'm sorry for how I reacted to everything. I didn't want it to end. Not really.'

He began to walk back to her, frowning. 'But you made it very obvious you didn't want me. Are you saying that you do now? You've changed your mind?'

His words were like tiny daggers stabbing at her heart. 'I always wanted you, you idiot. But I was scared. It went from a game, a battle of wills and a point to prove, to very serious, very quickly.' How else could she show him how she felt? Was this not enough?

'Matteo, I've been trying to prove that I'm worth something my whole life—it was hard, bloody hard, and there were times even I didn't believe it. But I learnt to fight for myself, I learnt not to rely on anyone, not to let anyone in because I just knew I'd get hurt in the end. And then you came along and I didn't need to try too hard with you because you seemed to accept me as I was—which was new and weird and exciting. And then I didn't know what to do. You took me by surprise—I needed to make space for you and I didn't want to let go of the safety blanket I'd shrouded myself in. My life was fine before you and your magnificent bottom came along, thank you very much, I wasn't expecting to fall in love with you...'

'You love...?' His eyes widened at her admission.

She placed a finger over his mouth. If she didn't say it all now, she might never say it. 'I felt frightened by the intensity of how I was feeling. My mum...she never wanted me around. Even now I'm of no use to her and I guess I got used to being on my own. But the thing is, I'm lost without you. I'm lost with you too, but that's okay... I'd kind of like us to be lost with each other. If you'll give me a second chance?'

He looked at her for a while. Took her finger from his lips and pressed a kiss onto the tip. 'I'm not lost at all, Ivy. I found you and you are worth more to me than everything else.'

'Oh, so good...'

But he still didn't look convinced. He wasn't. 'How do I know you mean it this time? How do I know you will not throw it all back in my face?'

Oh, so bad. Was he for real? Could he not see the love she knew was in her eyes? Could he not hear it in her voice? 'You want *more* than thirty thousand pounds, a massive show of support and a new dialysis machine? Really? That's not enough? This isn't enough? I'm not enough? I love you, Matteo. I don't know how else to show you. Please, believe me. I'm not Elizabetta. I'm not your father. I won't throw your love back at you. I don't know what else would prove to you how I feel.'

The crowds had all moved along, balloons bobbing in the distance, the park now silent except for the whistle of wind through the trees and a dull buzz from a hovering bee. And she was left standing with Matteo, alone, in a garden that smelt of sunshine and roses. Then she smiled to herself. She'd noticed them. Becca would be proud.

He looked away, at the balloons and the children and the banners. At the posters and the marquee. A slow smile flitted onto his lips as his gaze went from her eyes to her mouth. 'A kiss maybe?'

'Oh. Yes. Of course. Good idea.' She took a step closer, hardly daring to believe that this could be happening. Maybe he did believe her. His arms snaked round her waist and he dragged her to him. She bunched his work shirt into her fists, choking back the tears that were threatening. 'But how do you feel? About me? Us?'

'I love you more than anything. I told you already.'

She blinked, trying to remember. She would have remembered. 'When? When did you say that?'

'Our last kiss. I whispered it to you.'

'I wish I'd heard it.'

His mouth was close to her ear. 'I said, *Ti amo.*'

She tried it, to see how it felt. *'Ti amo,* Matteo. I love you.' Goddamn, it felt great, however she said it. Then she couldn't say anything else because the lump in her throat had got jammed there so tightly she could barely breathe. What little breath she did have left was whipped away by his kiss. A slow, gentle, heart-warming kiss that told her exactly how he felt.

He pulled away, a huge grin on his face. 'No more wars? No more games.'

'None.'

'Good.' His finger stroked the side of her cheek. 'So we have some catching up to do.'

'Oh, yes, the run… We'd better hurry up, we're going to be last.'

He shook his head, those dark eyes blazing with

desire, a smile that was at once innocent and dirty. 'I wasn't thinking about that. I want you so bad...'

'*Badly.*' She saw the flicker of a frown then the smile. Then the grimace. 'Oh, whatever, I don't care how you say it. Just keep on saying it... I want you right back.'

'You know, you will drive me crazy.' He held out his hand.

She took it, held on tight, promising to never let go. 'That sounds like a very good plan.'

* * * * *

MILLS & BOON®
Large Print Medical

December

Midwife...to Mum!	Sue MacKay
His Best Friend's Baby	Susan Carlisle
Italian Surgeon to the Stars	Melanie Milburne
Her Greek Doctor's Proposal	Robin Gianna
New York Doc to Blushing Bride	Janice Lynn
Still Married to Her Ex!	Lucy Clark

January

Unlocking Her Surgeon's Heart	Fiona Lowe
Her Playboy's Secret	Tina Beckett
The Doctor She Left Behind	Scarlet Wilson
Taming Her Navy Doc	Amy Ruttan
A Promise...to a Proposal?	Kate Hardy
Her Family for Keeps	Molly Evans

February

Hot Doc from Her Past	Tina Beckett
Surgeons, Rivals...Lovers	Amalie Berlin
Best Friend to Perfect Bride	Jennifer Taylor
Resisting Her Rebel Doc	Joanna Neil
A Baby to Bind Them	Susanne Hampton
Doctor...to Duchess?	Annie O'Neil

MILLS & BOON®
Large Print Medical

March

Falling at the Surgeon's Feet	Lucy Ryder
One Night in New York	Amy Ruttan
Daredevil, Doctor...Husband?	Alison Roberts
The Doctor She'd Never Forget	Annie Claydon
Reunited...in Paris!	Sue MacKay
French Fling to Forever	Karin Baine

April

The Baby of Their Dreams	Carol Marinelli
Falling for Her Reluctant Sheikh	Amalie Berlin
Hot-Shot Doc, Secret Dad	Lynne Marshall
Father for Her Newborn Baby	Lynne Marshall
His Little Christmas Miracle	Emily Forbes
Safe in the Surgeon's Arms	Molly Evans

May

A Touch of Christmas Magic	Scarlet Wilson
Her Christmas Baby Bump	Robin Gianna
Winter Wedding in Vegas	Janice Lynn
One Night Before Christmas	Susan Carlisle
A December to Remember	Sue MacKay
A Father This Christmas?	Louisa Heaton